Contents

THE ACCIDENTAL WIFE

Winner of the Eludia Award

Hidden River Arts offers the Eludia Award for a first book-length unpublished novel or collection of stories by a woman writer, age 40 or above. The Eludia Award provides $1000 and publication by Hidden River Publishing on its Sowilo Press imprint. The purpose of the prize is to support the many women writers who meet with delays and obstacles in discovering their creative selves.

Hidden River Arts is an interdisciplinary arts organization dedicated to supporting and celebrating the unserved artists among us, particularly those outside the artistic and academic mainstream.

THE
ACCIDENTAL
WIFE

stories

ORLA MᶜALINDEN

:::::::::::::::::::::::::::::::::::

SOWILO PRESS
Philadelphia   2016

Acknowledgements

Versions of the following stories have previously been published:

"Bleeding," *Number Eleven Magazine*, Issue 2, June 2013, www.numberelevenmagazine.com

"Breathing," *Wasafiri: International Contemporary Writing*, October 2013 (shortlisted for the Wasafiri New Writing Prize), www.wasafiri.org

"Bye Now," *A New Ulster*, Issue 17, February 2014; also previously published at SkyPen, www.skypen.co.uk, September 2013, and on the author's blog, November 2013

"Carphone, 1992," *Roadside Fiction*, Issue 4, June 2013, www.roadsidefiction.com; reprinted in *A New Ulster*, Issue 12, September 2013

"Control Zone" (nonfiction version), *Ragnarok,* Spring 2013 (second prize in the Valhalla Short Prose contest)

"Good Friends," *Stories for the Ear* (audio anthology), Kildare County Council, Ireland, October 2014

"The Quare Fella," *Wordlegs Magazine*, Issue 16, Winter 2013; also at Writing.ie, www.writing.ie/member-emerging-writers/orla-mcalinden

"The Visit," *The Ilanot Review*, Summer 2014 (nominated for The Pushcart Prize), http://ilanot.wordpress.com/the-visit/

Cover design by Miriam Seidel
Cover photographs: Coshkib Hill Farm, Ulster Folk Museum, Belfast, © Paul Shaw/Alamy Stock Photo; young girl, iStock.com/Linda Yolanda

Interior design and typography by P. M. Gordon Associates

Library of Congress Control Number: 2016946145
ISBN 978-0-9844727-7-2

SOWILO PRESS
An imprint of Hidden River Publishing
Philadelphia, Pennsylvania

To Barbara and John, and Ben and Nellie,
whose voices echo through this book

Author's Note

The characters, and the lives lived within this book, are works of fiction. Alo O'Donovan is not your father, nor mine; Joan is not your mother. However, the scenarios which fill these pages are familiar to my peers. We shared the same fears: the stranger in the yard, the late-night knock at the door, the child who leaves home in a school uniform and returns in a closed coffin. I have not told "your story" except to the extent that your story is also my story, and that the deeds of four dark decades have collectively become our story.

THE ACCIDENTAL WIFE

Strike

::::::

I T HAPPENED on the way to school.

One of the masked, hooded men rapped on the windscreen, while the others waited in a grim, silent semicircle. Joan struggled with the handle of the car window, tugging and winding. It was an old, beat-up Ford, one of Dominic's cast-offs. As so often happened, the window jammed, half up, half down.

The man beckoned with his index finger. "Out."

Joan gripped the door handle, and did a quick head count. There were seven men that she could see, maybe more behind. They did not wear balaclavas, that would be too honest, but they had scarves wrapped tightly round their lower faces and some had hoods pulled well down. She could not see one face clearly; here a wisp of reddish beard, here a splash of a livid strawberry birthmark popped up above the encircling fabric, but not enough. Not enough to say *yes, I could recognise this man.*

In the back seat, Rory whimpered softly. "What's happening, Mammy? Are these bad guys?" She glanced over her shoulder and smiled, reached back a comforting hand to stroke his hair. "Hush, pet, don't worry, we'll soon be on our way again."

Joan gave the window handle a brutal, final twist. Something inside the mechanism popped with an audible crack and the window slid down at last. Joan breathed again and sat back into her seat.

The man leaned his head into the vehicle, inches from Joan's face. His breath was fresh and minty, no hint of alcohol or tobacco, a God-fearing, clean-living man. The man carried no weapon, but in his right hand he held a placard aloft. Close up, it appeared that he had chosen the handle of a spade to support his flimsy sign, when a spindly length of bamboo would have sufficed. The six other men held placards too—*Ulster Workers Council, No power-sharing, General Strike, In God We Trust*—supported on long, strong timbers, broom handles and the like.

"Good mornin', madam, might I ask you where yer goin'?" The over-polite, civilised words were muffled slightly through the thickness of the woollen scarf around his mouth.

"Ask away, for all the good it'll do you." Joan's voice was as steady as his. "Ask away, man dear, I'm in no great hurry. I don't see a polis man with you. When the polis comes along, I'll answer any question he wants."

"The police? Sure, what would we want the police for, just a few friends and concerned citizens having a wee stand, and a wee chat, on the side of the road?"

"But yer not on the side of the road, sure yer not. You're in the middle of the road. You're blocking the Queen's highway, man. Very dangerous. Imagine if my foot slipped off the brake?"

Joan gunned the engine, ever so slightly; the idling car roared its protest for a moment. The man snapped his head out of the car and stepped back, but the six other men drew closer. One of them hefted his placard, studying the length of wood with curious intensity.

The spokesman came closer and leaned his elbow on the open sill of the window. "Now, now, madam, we don't want any wee misunderstandings. You just tell us where yer headin' off to, and we'll tell you if we think that's a good idea."

He smiled at Rory cowering in the back seat, the child's hands squirming under his knees, where he had put them to hide his trembling. The man smiled. "Would you like a day or two off school, son? Would you like to go home and play with your Lego?"

"Oh, so yer not blind, then?" Joan snapped. "I thought maybe you had trouble with your eyes, and you standing in the middle of the road, asking people stupid questions. You can see the child is in his school uniform, you can safely take a guess that we are headin' up to the school."

The man smiled and indicated his homemade placard. In wobbling, red felt-tip pen someone had patiently, neatly coloured in the words, *United Ulster Unionist Council, General strike. No! to Dublin. Smash Sunningdale.*

"Have you no radio, Missus? Have you no TV? Mebbe you don't know about the strike?" He smiled and scratched his neck, red and chafed from the woollen scarf. His fingernails were short and black-rimmed, the hands of a manual worker, like Dominic's hands at home on the farm. Hands of a man more used to doing than to speaking. A man who might, by now, have dragged Dominic out of the car and thrown him onto the silent, deserted roadway. That's why Dominic was at home.

:   :   :   :

"WOMAN, ARE YE CRAZY?" Dominic had roared, as she folded Rory's sandwiches into a small Tupperware with Paddington Bear on the lid. "You, of all people, going to school, today of all days, bringing down trouble on yer own head, and draggin' the chil' intil it? Let him stay at home, to hell."

She had placed the schoolbag over Rory's shoulder. "Me, of all people, what the fuck is that supposed to mean?" The child's head had snapped up in shock and he had gasped to hear Mammy say bad words. She'd pushed Rory out the front door, banging his hipbone off the wooden doorframe, but he'd had the sense not to howl, not to draw attention to himself and divert the rage streaming between his parents.

"You know well what I mean. Sure you're as Orange as half a' them bastards, with your Protestant ma hidin' away out here, sittin' in the front row at Sunday Mass and sendin' her wee accident to the Convent school, thinkin' we're all as green as we're cabbage-lookin'. Did she ever think she fooled anyone? Your ma was a Prod, you're half-a-Prod, this is not your fight and you're not draggin' my chil' intil it. Get back in the house."

Joan had thrust Rory sprawling onto the back seat of the battered, red Escort and slammed the door so the whole car shook. "Stay home safe, Dominic, don't put one foot outside them gates the day. This *is* my fight. I'm raised a Catholic, married a Catholic, I've a houseful a' wee taigs comin' up behind me. If I amn't Catholic enough for you, I'm sure as hell not Protestant enough for them uns out blocking the roads. Get out of my way, Dominic, we are goin' to school."

The car had started the first time, and in the mirror she had seen her husband spit on the ground, fists clenched. His words were said now, and could never be unsaid. She would deal with the words later.

:::::

THE MAN standing by Joan's car window stopped scratching and flicked the flakes of skin from under his nails. He had exhausted his script and now he was improvising. "Could I see your driving license, madam?"

Joan barked a hoarse, tense laugh. "My driving license? Are you out of yer tiny mind? I told you, when the polis get here, I'll answer any question they have." Her driving license was tucked into the sun visor, clearly visible. He need only reach in and take it. On the blue fabric cover of the small license-book was printed in flowing, black copperplate *Care, Courtesy, and Consideration on the road saves lives*. On the subject of illegal roadblocks, it remained silent.

A man stepped forward out of the pack and loomed over the vehicle, as broad as he was tall, powerful shoulders bulging inside a black, woollen funeral coat. "Never you mind about the driving license, Jackie boy. Thon's Joan McCann, Dominic McCann's woman, from Drumnagort."

Joan flashed a bright smile at the new man's hidden face. "Ach, Sam, lad. How's about you? Did yer father ever get that big tree stump shifted outta the back meadow? The one Dominic lent him the JCB digger for? Tell yer Da, Joan McCann was askin' for him."

The man known as Jackie shot a furious glance in Sam's direction, and Sam shuffled his feet and stepped back to rejoin the small knot of men a few feet away.

"Listen, now." The voice had risen in pitch, sounding uncertain for the first time. "If you drive into town and bring that child to school, we'll have to burn the car. And the school will be closed, anyway, by order of Dr Paisley . . ."

Joan pulled out her purse and rummaged in the secret pocket, pulling out a crisp five pound note. "Christ, that's great news!" She forced the bank note into the man's unresisting hand. "That's great altogether, I'm nagging my man for a new car this six months past. Sure, you can see her windas hardly open, and half the time the bloody thing doesn't start. I'll leave her in Market Street, and I'll give you twenty minutes. Throw a match in the petrol tank for me, good lad." She released the handbrake and pressed, ever so gently, on the accelerator. "You'll be doing me a great turn there, I won't forget you, nor Sam Gilmartin, neither."

The car nosed gently through the baffled protesters, and Joan watched the men stare blankly at her emergency fiver, her running-away money. It was gone now, gone on the first day that she had ever considered using it.

At St Brigid's school, Daniel Byrne looked up and sighed when he saw her. Joan grinned and called briskly, "How's about ya, Master Byrne, lovely weather we're having. I'll just drop Rory over to his classroom."

"Mrs McCann, for goodness sake, what are you doing here?" Daniel's shoulders slumped and his voice abruptly dropped the fuss and effeminacy of forty years of primary-school teaching. "I mean, Joan, for God's sake, how did you even *get* here?"

"I just had a wee chat with some polite young men above at the crossroads and they waved me through, nice as pie. How did you get here?"

Dan Byrne heaved a lungful of air and drew his hands across his face, although there was no sweat there to wipe away. "I walked, Joan, and I walked at five in the morning, before the birds started singing, and I don't know how or when I'll get home."

He pulled Joan into a corner, leaving Rory to kick a stone around the deserted playground. "Joan, you're a lucky woman. You ran into the early squad, it's half eight in the morning, for Christ's sake. Who's out there now? I'll tell you: the clean-livers, the teetotallers, the lunatics who think this is about politics, and God, and that aul' bitch in Buckingham Palace. I tell you, Joan, you try that trick again at three o'clock in the afternoon, when the drink has been flowing and the thugs and hired muscle are finally awakened up outta their pits and you have a quare shock coming to you."

"You want me to take the child home? Is that what you're saying? You're bowing down to that pack of bastards and you're closing the school?"

Daniel rubbed his faded, grey eyes and pinched the bridge of his nose, where the heavy National Health Service glasses left two angry, red indentations. "No, Joan, the school is open. Just no pupils, that's all. The school is open until the Ministry of Education tells me it's closed. I take my orders from the Minister, not from Paisley nor the Orange Order. The school is open. I have plenty of paperwork to get on with."

"And Sarah McMonagle, has she plenty of paperwork too? And Anne Kelly? Are they sitting in their classrooms in front of empty desks, when Rory is here, keen and waiting for an education?"

"No, Joan. No pupils today. No female teachers. Just me. On account of the *no water*, you know? We had a burst water pipe last night. No water for flushing the toilets. No water in the canteen, for boiling the potatoes. No water, so no pupils. No female teachers, neither, not with no water in the toilets, you can see how it is."

"A burst pipe?" Joan's laugh was a bitter, face-twisting snarl. "A burst pipe? In May? Man dear, you're telling me, the school is closed to pupils because you've *no water*?"

"That's right."

"And when do you imagine the pipe will be fixed?"

"Oh, I'd say the school will be open again the day after the Orange calls off the strike." He winked. It was a badly judged gesture.

"Dan Byrne, you're as yella as a duck's foot. You're chicken to the core."

He drew himself up, ran a hand through the grey wisps of his comb-over, his formal, stiff manner returning at once. "Missus McCann, I have two hundred pupils to think about. So far, fifteen pupils have turned up. Fair play to you. Fifteen parents, all women. Well done, you've made your point. I will be here every day, come hell or high water, no pun intended, until the pipe is mended. Go home, Missus McCann. And don't come back."

At the crossroads, Joan waved and smiled, and kept her foot firmly down, a steady thirty miles an hour as she passed Sam and Jackie and their friends. The men leapt for the ditch at the last possible moment. Rory lay hidden from view in the footwell, *in school.*

"Go and help your daddy in the milking parlour, love," Joan said, as they stepped out into the farmyard.

She scalded the teapot and wet the tea. *You're as Orange as half a' them bastards.* She poured a cup of tea, rattling a symphony with the spoon and saucer in her unsteady hand. *You, of all people.* She took a sip and grimaced as the hot cup stuck to her lower lip for a moment. *You're half-a-Prod.* The words of her husband and her late mother merged and blended, they rang in her head. *What can't be cured, must be endured.* Joan started to shake, the tea slopped over her skirt, the expensive Sunday skirt that she had selected carefully that morning. She shook for three days.

Control Zone

: : : : :

AUNTIE NORA hurts your hand—you know now how a bullock feels when Daddy slams its neck in the cattle crush. When the bullock struggles, Daddy rams his strong fingers up its nostrils and gives its head a mighty shake. You do not resist; Auntie Nora might shake you too. She drags you onward, *stop dilly-dallying.* Sometimes Rory puts your hands into the vice-grip in the workshed at home, when you are playing Spanish Inquisition. You are always the heretic, Rory is always the monk, but he does not hurt you too much, turning the screw, not so much that you run to Daddy, a traitor, a super-grass like the ones in the Diplock courts. Rory is careful when he twists the vice; he is only messing.

But Auntie Nora is not messing; with a knuckle-whitening grasp, she marches you towards the city centre. She has parked the car on the outskirts of town, in a dingy, rubble-filled car park, supervised by a melancholy man in a rain-soaked mac. No vehicles are allowed in the Control Zone. Damp, hunch-shouldered pedestrians file joylessly into Belfast. One by one, they pass through black, wrought-iron turnstiles, past coils of razor wire, supervised by British soldiers with AK-47s.

With a dismissive muzzle-flick, a red-nosed corporal silently indicates Nora's bag. Your face blazes and hot, suppressed rage twists your guts like a dishcloth in Mammy's strong fingers.

This boy, this Brit, who does he think he is? What does he think Auntie Nora is carrying in her prized canvas shopping bag from Harrod's, posted over by Auntie Deirdre in Luton? You are insulted, but also cringing with embarrassment. Drifts of fresh and used Kleenex float out from the cavernous bag, to be whipped away by the vicious gale that howls through Belfast's turnstiles. The Kleenex is followed by cigarette packets, some open, some full, and dozens of half-used Bic lighters. Diaries, lipsticks, memorial cards, photos of long-dead relatives, and of Pope John Paul II, and of you, beaming out under your First Communion veil.

Why does she not clean out her handbag in advance of this unsecret ritual?

Today the sentry is particularly bloody-minded; he opens all the sealed packets of cigarettes, pulling out the gold foil and inspecting the fags, as if Auntie Nora could conceal a bomb within the confines of twenty Benson and Hedges.

You wish she would give up the fags, like Mammy is always telling her. You have been trapped in Nora's car for seventy miles and she has smoked incessantly all the way from Omagh. Nora wafts along in a fog; your throat itches and your eyes brim with tears.

You hate travelling in Nora's car. She makes you sit in the back seat. You can't open your window in case her ash, or her discarded butt, flies back in on top of you. She drives like a granny. When Daddy hurtles you through the country lanes of Tyrone, the roads are full of *stupid bastards* and *ignorant cyarns*, your tummy leaps and soars as you wheeee over the little humpy-backed bridges. When Daddy stamps on the brakes he flings out his left arm, rock-solid and powerful from his hard work on the farm. You feel safe when your chest slams into his arm. He will always catch you. You wish you were at home with Daddy instead of trailing round Belfast with Auntie Nora.

The radio in Auntie Nora's car is permanently tuned to Radio Ulster; if you ripped off the knob and threw it out the window, would she notice? She tuts and clucks along with the headlines and makes the sign of the cross at the naming of each new murder. *Daddy* lets you tune the radio in his station wagon to Radio Caroline, and you sit in the car in the busy farmyard with your tape recorder, trying to catch the soul and spirit of this jungle-bunny music that Daddy does not allow in the house, but the DJ always spoils it by talking over the intro. Whenever Daddy sees a British Army checkpoint on the road ahead, he flicks the station over to Radio Éireann and blasts out diddly-eye Irish traditional music. *Morning, officer,* he says, as the Irish music rages out through the open window into the pelting rain, *lovely day for ducks.* When you are safely through the checkpoint, he switches back to *Boney M*, and he sings the chorus in a whisper, so that little Francie will not hear and tell Mammy—*There's a dead Brit in the rain, tra la la la la. Dead Brit in the rain. Traaaa, la la la la.*

Women are no fun, not like men, not like Daddy. Women are only *wash your hands, wet the tea, wipe the dishes.* Women never play jokes. On Frank's birthday, Daddy has wrestled his new toy gun from him. Daddy is watching the *Scene around Six* news programme and suddenly he is howling with laughter. You look, you giggle. The boys are shrieking. Daddy is the loudest—it is his special laugh, his Laurel and Hardy roar, the one that makes you worry that it might be possible to die with laughter. Daddy has shot Ian Paisley with Frank's new gun, the dart is suckered to Paisley's forehead while he's roarin' and gulderin' at the newscaster. *Right between the eyes,* Daddy bellows, *take that, ya wee Orange cyarn. Hell's curse on ye.*

Mammy rushes in from the kitchen, suds dripping from her steaming red hands. You wait for her to say something, to ruin everything, to make Daddy sink back sullenly in his chair. She looks at the TV. You hold your breath. Suddenly, incredibly, she is whooping with the rest of you, *good enough for him, the rotten wee blirt,* she says, and her voice is kind. *Good shot, Dominic,* and your heart is going to explode. And you love Daddy even more than before, for making Mammy laugh again, and you slide down in the space between his big, smelly feet and you lean your head against his hard, knobbly knee and you wonder if it is possible to die from loving someone too much. There are so many ways to die: bomb–blast–bad–luck, hole–in–the–head–personal, machine–gun–riddle. Hatred. Love?

::::

BUT NOW you are with Auntie Nora and Daddy is far away. Through the turnstiles at last and released onto the street. Armed soldiers and police with their backs against walls, never resting their flickering, darting eyes. The men are so big, so bulky in their bulletproof vests, the RUC ladies are dainty in comparison, though they are surely at just as much risk. Why would anyone, even a Protestant, want to be a lady cop? Why would anyone want to come to Belfast? Why could you not have stayed at home, with Daddy?

Every doorway, every store, holds its own security man. Entering Anderson and McAuley's or Robinson and Cleaver's involves rooting though the handbag again, to varying degrees of officiousness. You start at ground level, and work upwards through each floor of these massive stores; Windsmoor, Eastex, Steilmann for coats, Bally for shoes. There is no shop like this in Omagh. These shops might be in London, or Paris, except for the handbag rummaging.

You sit on a red velvet chair in the changing room, itchy and hot. Auntie Nora frowns when you swing your legs and places a hand on your knee. Auntie Nora does not say *quit yer friggin' wrigglin' about*, Auntie Nora says, *don't be a silly sausage, Gemma*. Your scowl deepens with every half hour.

At last Nora has finished her shopping—she doesn't need any more clothes, anyway. Mammy says Nora has more rig-outs than the Queen of England. Mammy says Nora has more money than sense. Sometimes, Mammy says Nora is the *only* one with any sense; no husband, no kids, good job. Mammy sounds sad when she says this, sometimes she sounds angry.

You stand in a queue in the dreary café on the top floor of Robinson and Cleaver's until a table becomes free. Nora detects some unsavoury fragment, left behind on the formica by the careless smearing of the semi-clean cloth. The waitress is recalled imperiously, to clean the table . . . *properly this time*. Further humiliation. You sink lower in your seat.

"Well, Gemma. Did Mammy and Daddy vote in the election last week? Did you get a day off school?" You shrug. Nora should know that your school is never closed for the election; it is the same school she went to, in the same village. Auntie Nora should know that the polling station is always in the Protestant school. Carol and Pauline got a day off school, *and* they don't have to give up sweets for Lent, *and* they don't have to go to Confession. But, of course, they are going to hell when they die so it all evens out in the end.

"Did Mammy and Daddy vote for the SDLP, Gemma?" Auntie Nora smiles, she has bought you a slice of chocolate cake, the taste blends with the taste of her cigarette smoke and the smell of the ashtray. After cake, she is going to buy your Confirmation outfit, she is going to buy you a hat and shoes, you are lucky to have rich Auntie Nora for your godmother.

"Did they? Did they vote for the SDLP?" You shrug again. How would you know? You spear a chunk of cake on your fork, it is good cake. If you make Auntie Nora angry she might not buy you any shoes, or she might get you a tartan kilt with a big safety pin for your Confirmation—she likes tartan kilts, even though they are for little girls.

"Mammy said she was voting for the Alliance. Daddy went mad. He said it was to be expected from the *spawn of that stuck-up, turncoat bitch*." Auntie Nora gasps and draws her chair closer, her long, trembling ash falls onto the table. Grown-ups are always at this business, always asking questions, but they don't want the truth. They all want a different answer and nobody ever tells you which one they want. When Mother Benignus at choir practice asks you who protected you last summer when you fell out of the hayshed loft and only broke your arm, you say *It was our blessed Virgin Mother*, but when Mrs Richardson in the Post Office asks, you tell her *It was Our Lord and Saviour, Jesus Christ*. You don't know how you know that proddies need different answers from

Catholics, nobody ever tells you anything. You have to work it all out for yourself.

Auntie Nora is silent and still and you realise that you have said a bad word. *Bitch.* Now she definitely might not buy the shoes, you might have to wear last year's sandals and your toes are sticking out at the top. You try to think of something soothing to say.

"I think Mammy was joking about voting for the Alliance?" It might have been one of those grown-up jokes that are not very funny. The person telling the joke laughs, but in a harsh, splintered-glass kind of way and the other person doesn't laugh at all, just goes red, or bangs his fist on the table or shakes the house as he slams out through the door. It must have been one of those jokes, you suppose.

"Never mind, pet," Auntie Nora says, but you can tell that she is still cross with you, because her eyes are wrinkled, and she is sniffing and blowing her nose to hide it. You plough on with the repair job, to make her forget about the B-word.

"I think Daddy might have voted for Sinn Fein? I think maybe Bobby Sands? Is that the right man?" You finish the cake quickly, just in case. Auntie Nora takes a quare gunk at you, her eyes pop out like a goldfish. "Houl' yer whisht, Gemma. Name-a-God." Auntie Nora is really rattled now, she is talking like a normal person, she has taken the marbles out of her mouth, like Daddy says.

She glances around quickly, as if she is looking for a friend, but all the tables near you are empty now and the waitress is keeping a wide berth after the *properly this time* incident. Nora drags hard on her fag. Suddenly she looks tired, even though she has her dark-orange makeup on, as usual. "No, pet, Bobby Sands is dead this two years past. Never mind. Never mind that I asked and don't bother mentioning it to Daddy. Or Mammy."

Her lips are thin and her nostrils are aflare like a frightened pony that will not walk past an old plastic bag flapping in a hedge. You have worried her, but you really don't know how.

Later, she spots a blouse with a missing button. Bad luck, it is your size. Presenting the garment at the till, she negotiates a reduced price for the spoiled item. You hide behind a rail, disowning this supremely embarrassing woman.

She will sew on another button, and in two weeks' time she will stand at the altar with her hand on your shoulder and present you to the Bishop. She will forgive you your mistake. Whatever it was.

The Reluctant Farmer

:::::

RORY SLICKED the moisture off his sweating shoulders. Hot. It was bloody, brilliantly hot. He was lucky to be young in this rare, hot summer. The sun shone from May until August.

His body was hard from labour, golden brown all over, no farmer's tan this year, it was just too hot for clothes. Only under his greying, fraying Jockey shorts was his skin the traditional Irish colour—the exact shade of the underbelly of a fish. Last week, at the county show, he had met a town girl, along for the novelty of the rural day out. She had caught his eye several times. She circled closer and closer to stall 86, where he was inspecting a new electric fence. A monotonous, cracking sound punctuated their short conversation, the air acrid with the smell of the blackened, raw potato being electrocuted forty or fifty times per minute.

"Jesus!" she said, when he opened his big, thick Tyrone mouth. "I thought you were Italian or Spanish, or something. You're brown as a berry."

He blushed dull-red. It was the nicest thing a girl had ever said to him. Italian, Spanish, even English—anything was better than Northern Irish. And Northern Irish Catholic to boot. "You'd be a long time waiting to see a Spaniard round here. Why would anyone with a say in the matter come to live in this shithole, when we can't get out of it fast enough?"

He had acquired his tan slogging on the farm all summer, under the careful, critical eye of his father, always on the lookout for a chance to complain, to compare, to contrast.

His father. Dominic. Poor, hard-done-by Dominic. Dominic sighing and lamenting. *What did I do to be cursed with such a shower of useless bastards?* Or *ungrateful bastards?* Or *careless, throughother bastards?*

Auntie Nora tutted and sighed each time she heard her brother at this business. Rory's mother, Joan, had perfected the art of ignoring Dominic entirely.

Today, late August, Rory sweated by the hall door, palms sticky, heart pounding, waiting for the postman. He had done well in his O-level exams at the Sacred Heart College in Omagh, he knew that already. The question was, how well?

An envelope slid through the letterbox, quietly flopping onto the mat. It lay there, like a pipe bomb tossed with careful malice into a playground. "Pick me up," it seemed to say. "Play with me. We'll have fun, until I detonate."

Rory yelled up the stairs, "I got my results."

Joan was changing the linen on the beds. She did it weekly. *Mother-a-God, woman, you'll wash us away*, grumbled Dominic at the same, weekly, interval. *Do you think I'm made of money? It's no friggin' wonder the twin-tub washer packed up.* He glared at the front-loading Hotpoint washing machine. *Damn the washing machine was ever needed in this house afore you came intil it. My mother scrubbed the linen in the scullery, and once a month was enough for the sheets in them days.*

Once a month? Joan's voice soared up into her highest, most aggressive register. *Catch yerself on. Once a month, and the cut of you, coming in stinkin' every day, unwashed from one Sunday's Mass 'til the next. Weeks I do be prayin' for a mid-week funeral, for you to clean yerself up. Once a month? The sheets'd be like the bloody Turin Shroud.*

Rory's mother did not come downstairs as he weighed the brown envelope with both shaking hands. His father was in the milking parlour. He did not call his father in; sixteen years of rebuffs had taught him never to go seeking Dominic out. He stood a moment longer, savouring the feeling. Anticipation and dread in equal measures. It was the first time he had ever received a letter with his printed name peering out through a cellophane window. His future was riding on its contents.

"What'd you get?" Joan called, as she battled a recalcitrant pillow case.

His grandfather's letter opener lay on a fake mahogany table beside the door, next to the tightly tethered telephone. A lot of crises had developed round that table. Sick relatives, overdue bills, complaints from the Co-op about the quality of Dominic's milk—all such dramas were enacted within the tight confines of the hallway. The harsh jangle of the phone or the crisp, precise slitting of the envelope, the unfolding rustle, the bitter litany of his father's complaint, recrimination, or, rarely, jubilation riddled with twisted satisfaction: *Johnny Devlin is after getting his herd locked up with tuberculosis; has three clear tests to get through before he can sell them calves now. He'll be needin' to buy a lot more than ten acres of silage off of us, if he's to feed thon crowd through the whole winter. Couldn't have happened to a nicer man; thon miserable wee get. Hell slap it up him.*

No, Rory was not going to sully his envelope with his grandfather's letter opener, its stiletto blade worn thin from three lifetimes of use. He ripped his letter open with a ragged thumbnail and extracted the form.

"What'd you get?" echoed his mother's voice, exasperated now.

"Nine As and a B . . ." Rory kept his face straight and his voice steady and unconcerned. "Nine As and a B." He called up the stairs, standing alone, waiting.

"What did you get the B in?"

Joan went back to her folding, smoothing, and patting.

"Ring Auntie Nora. You needn't ring anyone else. Nora will spread the word faster than the *Tyrone Courier*, and then it won't be seen to come from us."

Rory made a few extra calls too. Spreading the word. On the whole, his friends were happy enough. No one had made such a hames of the exams that they needed to sit Fifth Year again. That was the sum of his friends' ambition, to move up to Sixth Year or out of the school altogether, to hell or any other place that would take them.

"Jesus, Rory, ya big fucken swot. Ya big genius-head on ya. You were always a big teacher's suck. What did yer Ma say? My Ma's been on the phone three-quarters of an hour already about my six Cs, and never mention the two Es!"

"Yeah, it's party central here. They're out there now, killing the fatted calf. Sure the Da has bought a bottle of champagne and sprayed it all over the milking parlour, like Ayrton Senna. The cows are licking up puddles of champagne out of the feeders."

"Christ, Rory, it's a long way from champagne your Da was reared, with the big gurney Pioneer-head on him. Gave up the drink for the sake of *his* miserable bastard of a father languishin' in purgatory, I suppose?"

"Too fuckin' tight to buy his round, you mean," laughed Rory. "I'll see you down McConville's later on, they're sure to serve us, today of all days, and if they don't we'll get a bottle of vodka somehow . . . maybe your Meabh might get it for us . . . ?"

And in McConville's that night, the master plan had been hatched. A weekend camping in Cranfield. It was a stony aul' spot and the tough, coarse grass atop the dunes was full of pishmires, fierce black ants that rushed out to nip at the ankles and shins disturbing their colonies, but it was the seaside, nonetheless. Vinnie had a four-man tent and they all had sleeping bags. They could survive on Irwin's plain loaves, ham, and cider. They would not starve for a long weekend.

"We fucken deserve it, for the love of God! Didn't we all do brilliant? I've got twenty quid."

"I've a tenner, I'll get a few bottles of Blackthorn."

"No, Strongbow is cheaper than Blackthorn. Or Buckfast, best of all, so sweet it tastes the same comin' back up as it did goin' down."

Rory joined in enthusiastically, though he knew he was going nowhere.

The silage was in, clamped, and covered. The hay was made. It was perfect hay, the first year ever in his life when there had been no madcap scramble, no last-minute, panicked dash to bale, with the dark storm clouds rushing in from the West. Even

Dominic could find no fault with it. "Thanks be to God, the hay saved and housed before the end of July, and plenty left over to sell."

Rory could easily be spared from the land for a few days, but it was never going to happen. Neither Joan nor Dominic had any time for messing around. "Send them all back to school, to hell," roared Dominic periodically. "Did the Ministry of Education never hear about the invention of the tractor? Sure, I'd have done in two days what it took my father, and me, and the three brothers, two weeks to do when I was a child. Eight weeks holidays? Lying on their arses like big, fat churns a-dryin'. Hell's curse it! I've a right mind to plough the three-corner meadow and set them to pick the stones out of it, just to get them outta my sight for a few days."

Rory and his brothers scarcely breathed. Their father was nearly capable of doing it out of spite, though the field was not due re-seeding for three or four years yet.

No, Rory would not be lying on the sand in Cranfield. Not this year. Not ever. Unless . . .

Yes, he would do it quickly. They would never know. They would not find out until the camping was over, until it was too late to stop him. Then there would be raving, door-slamming, table-thumping, but that was nothing new.

"Da . . ." He started the following night at the dinner table. The blinds were open, and the windows. A brown, sticky fly-paper hung at the opening, liberally studded with victims, some still struggling. The warm air twirled the long spiral, a gruesome murder-machine, round and round, like the bit of a slow drill. Joan puffed in the heat, but the new potatoes were firm and floury, and his Da's plate was heaped high, glistening with large slabs of melting butter. Now was as good a time as any.

"Da, you know, I've been thinking. Maybe you're right. I mean, I've proved my point. Okay, so I got the nine As and all that, but I think mebbe you're right. I mean, what's the point of goin' back to school, just for the sake of it? Mebbe I *will* go straight to Greenmount and do the farming certificate."

Dominic struggled. He opened and closed his mouth several times before speaking. Joan was silent, with her knife still wedged in the butter dish, unheeded.

"Jesus," thought Rory, "He's going to say something nice. *Well done* maybe. Or *good man, yourself.* Something?"

"Well, Rory, just do whatever the fuck you want to . . . you always do anyway."

It sounded like a kick in the crotch, a slap in the face, but Rory knew his father better than that. Dominic was pleased, and he was victorious, and he had no intention of showing it.

Pressing on, cautious, tactful, choosing words with care, Rory explained how he had made his decision yesterday, listening to Paddy, and Vinnie, and Eoghan, and their big plans for independence. Dominic nodded, listening intently. Paddy was for his father's shop. Vinnie was for an apprenticeship with an electrician, he had scraped the C he needed in both Maths and Science. Eoghan was going back to school alright, but only because he couldn't find anything better to do.

"Keep him off the dole queue," mumbled Rory. "It's not like he has a farm or anything useful he could be doing."

And they were going on a camping trip . . . hitching to Cranfield . . . no big money involved . . .

Silently, deftly, Joan cleared the table and Rory and Dominic somehow acquired steaming triangles of apple tart. The jug of milk brought in daily from the parlour, often with a stray blade of fresh, green grass floating in it, had been carefully skimmed. The prized top-of-the-milk now swilled gently round the saucers, sweetening the tart. Dominic was dismissive of the pasteurised, homogenised product his customers at the Maybrook Dairy Co-op produced and sold on to city slickers. *The shop-bought milk is fit for nothing. It doesn't even colour the tay*, he declared, as if daring the family to disagree. The cream on the tart was no accident, no coincidence. Rory glanced surreptitiously at his mother. There was the tiniest hint of a smile on her pinched lips. She was on his side. The shame of the B forgotten; for once he was doing the right thing, obeying his father, keeping the peace.

"D'you know what, Rory? You should go with them." Dominic leaned back, expansive, the lord of the manor. "You should head off to Cranfield for a couple of days. You'll have precious little time for that kind of bolloxology after you start Greenmount. Get it out of your system."

"Jesus, Da, are you sure? What about paintin' the doors and the window frames?"

"Don't question me, Rory, or I'll question myself, change me mind, and that'll be the end of it. Go on your holiday. I'll do the windows a damn sight better than a throughother hallion like you, anyway. Be scrapin' paint off the glass for a year after you."

Rory fled out to the haggard, clutching his victory. Paddy, Vinnie, and Eoghan had better be ready to go tomorrow. They couldn't delay. They couldn't wait even one week. Rory had no idea when the letter would come from Monsignor Malone, confirming the A-level exam place that Rory had already accepted that afternoon, in his secret meeting in the Principal's office.

"Well done, Rory, the star of the school." The old priest's wattles had waggled as he gloated over Rory's precious results paper. "Wait 'til we get your picture in the *Chronicle*, telling everyone about the three As you'll be getting in a year or two. Good man! Looking forward to September already, I suppose?"

"No pictures in the paper, Father, we're not really that kind . . ."

"Alright, Rory—you're the boss—for today, anyway. Modesty is a virtue, I suppose."

Rory slipped out of the school gates and back to the farm, pedalling furiously. His father had not even noticed his hour-long absence. Rory would be back in school in September if it killed him.

The Visit

::::::

IN THE SECONDS before the visitor pulls a balaclava over his five o'clock shadow, you already know he is bad news. A solitary figure slouching up the long farm path, no friendly wave, no shouted greeting. Skin-tight denim, *drainpipes* your father would have called them. No dungarees, no boiler suit, you know this is not the unrecognised younger son of a neighbour come to borrow a half pound of staples for a barbed-wire fence.

Just before his face swims into focus, he pauses and pulls on the mask, taking all your attention, and you gasp in amazement as two other wraiths materialise from the shadows behind you.

Strangers on your land, in your yard. How strange are they? Let's find out.

"Dia daoibh," you say, strong and loud. "May God and Mary be with you," replies the first stranger; the words in the Irish language roll off his lips without thought, as automatic as the responses at Mass on Sunday. If you had intoned "The Lord be with you," he would have chanted back "And also with you." The man behind you to your left is more fluent still; "God's blessing upon the work" is his reply. The third man is silent.

Before, you knew nothing about your visitors. Now you know something. Catholic, Republican, Catholic-educated, Belfast accents. They might be graduates of the University of Long Kesh, where all the Republican prisoners only speak Irish, thwarting their Unionist prison guards, clinging desperately to this hint of dignity. IRA, INLA, IPLO, someone like that. The bulges in the men's coats are more obvious now; they have shifted their stance to bring the outline of the weapons into sharp relief against their cheap, nylon bomber jackets, but they have not produced them. Yet.

You are alone on the farm. Where is Baby? He is locked in the shed and you are glad he is safe. You have played many a good game with Baby, but you do not want to play it now.

When the Jehovah's Witnesses call to the farm, you always give them five minutes to talk. Five minutes is not too long to ask of any man. When the time has elapsed, you gently suggest that you will return to your labours, that they will go home. Two minutes later, if their stiff, black overcoats have not folded back into the red Datsun Cherry, you interrupt them. *Sorry, lads, I need to feed my little dog.* At the first sound of his name, Baby comes charging into the front yard. Saliva drools from his powerful chops and splatters on the ground. Jehovah's friends gasp or cry out as the Dobermann slips and slides to a halt, claws grating beside your Wellington boot. The pamphlets drop to the ground as the men struggle back into the small car, and you pick the papers up and hand them back smiling. *Sorry, lads, Baby hates waiting for his meal.*

Yes, you are glad the dog is locked up. These trigger-happy city boys will shoot him at first sight, before the first rich, bowel-loosening bay escapes his throat, and they will almost certainly make a mess of the shot, no clean death that a noble animal such as Baby deserves.

You are alone.

The men are slow to speak, they are out of their milieu. You have noted the involuntary wince, the twitch of disgust as Number One planted his shiny, black shoe into a barely crusted cow-pat on the laneway. Such impractical footwear, *winkle-pickers* your father would have called them.

They do not intend to kill you—you would be dead by now. Why would they kill you, one of their own, minding your business, bothering no one? What do they want?

At length, Number Three speaks, the singsong, nasal accent you have heard on the nightly news for two decades now, detailing the litany of woe; hard vowels, missing consonants, no country softness in this voice. "Now, Mr O'Donovan, we're here for a tractor and a dung-spreader. No need for any unpleasantness. A wee donation to the war effort, is all."

"The war effort, lads? But I'm not at war. A wee mistake, maybe? Maybe we'll all go back to our business and forget this wee misunderstanding?"

Number Three replies from the closeness of your right elbow. He does not touch you, but he is close, so close. "Not at war, Mr O'Donovan? The country is at war. The machinery will be put to good use, against the enemies of the Irish Republican Army."

"Enemies, you say? Yes, enemies. Farmers have many enemies, boys. Drought is my enemy and more so the endless rain and inundation. Lack of fodder following a wet summer is my battle, and the winter frost that turns the poached fields to rutted iron is my nemesis. I have no human foe, unless you mean the men in the Co-op who set the price for the milk so low that I can bare squeeze a living from the good land my father left me. I think you have come to the wrong place."

Numbers One and Two gawp and titter at you. Their mouths are open, *catching flies* your father called it. They glance uneasily to their leader for guidance. Slowly, and with menace, he claps his hands together, a bitter ovation. A thick gob of tobacco-brown phlegm lands on the concrete half an inch from your boot, preceding his words, calm, measured. "All well and good there, Hamlet. Ten outta ten for the composition, nice use of vocabulary there, yer teachers must be proud of you. They might be prouder still if you did your duty, and gave us the weapons we need to progress the war. Nathin' has been said yet that can't be unsaid."

In the small haggard beside the house a full line of washing flutters in the wind. The empty trouser legs and the flapping shirts bring into sharp recall a woodcut you saw long ago in an old book, a gibbet, its swinging, decaying scraps of bird-pecked humanity and wind-torn clothing blurred indistinctly into one.

Will you end up as a propaganda woodcut for a new generation, a photo in tomorrow's *Irish News*, a misshapen heap on a wheeled gurney on the bedtime news programme?

Under the laden clothesline a swoop of swallows, a hundred strong, frantically pecks, seeking worms, seeds, roots, anything that will sustain them on their journey back to Africa, away out of this mad hellhole. You know that any moment now, this massed gathering of rats on wings will take fright and take flight and, with a sound like the rattle of distant machine gun fire, will wheel up and away over your heads. You know that the visitors will jump and flinch, *taking their eye off the ball*, your father called it. If you are to take a chance, a fight or flight, it must be then.

"What time is it, boys?" Whatever is to happen, it must happen before Cormac comes cycling back from the Sacred Heart College in Omagh. What time is it? You know that if the boy comes home, you are lost. You know that if the men speak to your motherless son, if they casually touch one inch of his precious skin, or ruffle his hair in jest, you are lost.

You see it unfold in your mind's eye in slow motion, a premonition of the certainty of things to come. The man reaches out to touch your child, to take his bicycle from him, to inspire him in this heroic adventure against the enemies of God, motherland, and nature. You see yourself pivot and turn. Your teak-hard fist falls, like the sledgehammer you wielded all day yesterday, against the skull of this frail city weakling. Number Two you take down with a kick to the back of the knee, stamping and grinding your heel into his face, crushing his Belfast whine with your toe on his windpipe. Number One is lifted from the ground by the impact of your shoulder, massive from five decades of bullock-wrestling. Or else he has managed to extract his gun by now and has ended you. Either way, dead or in prison, murdered or murderer, you leave the boy behind, alone. Orphan.

Whatever is to happen must happen soon.

"Mr O'Donovan, we don't have all day. There is an easy way and a hard way. We need the keys. Giz the keys, Mr O'Donovan, and then take a wee sit-down in a chair with a hankie in yer mouth for a few hours. It's not much to ask."

You know that these men have never set foot on a farm before. It is no easy matter for a novice to hitch a muck-spreader to a tractor, working by instinct, one toe on the accelerator, the length of the body at full stretch, twisted and hoisted, head out the rear window. If you are clever, and brave, this could work out.

"The keys are in my pocket, boys. I won't give them to you. I daresay you will be able to take them, eventually." No one has drawn a gun yet, but the faceless men are sighing and flexing their fingers. Whatever happens, you must not get shot. You must not go to hospital with a *six-pack*, bullets lodged in your knees, elbows, and ankles. You must get away with a clean deception.

"Alo! Quit acting the fuckin' maggot. Giz the keys, and you won't get hurt. Three armed men against one? No need to act the fuckin' hero, no blame on an innocent farmer tied up and threatened by three masked men with guns."

No more *Mr O'Donovan*, then, is that good or bad? you wonder.

"Lads, I feel sure it won't be necessary to get the armoury out. What would people say? Shooting one of your own? On his own land, leaving a child orphaned? No, lads, there's nothing to be gained by shooting me that can't be obtained with a few slaps."

Number Two is twitching now; impatience reeks off him like steam off fresh dung on a frosty morning behind the cows on their slow walk to the parlour. "I'll cover you, get on with it," he says, producing a sawn-off. He holds the gun surprisingly still. You were expecting a bad case of nerves, the gun barrel to execute frail, trembling circles in his shaking hands, but he is steady as a rock. He has pointed a gun at a man before.

You stand like a statue as the first blow sinks into your solar plexus. You will not fight back—it is essential not to get shot—but you are hard and strong as a bull in his prime; this is not going to be quick. You finally sink to your knees as the blows rain down one after another. Your eye is closing fast. A concerto of kicks plays out upon your torso, ringing dull in your ears, mingling with the sounds of the men's demands.

They are wary, afraid to put their hands in your pockets. Is it a trap? Are you going to spring back to life from your bloodied mess, like the hero in a B movie, and turn the tables? You know you are not, you are not acting, you are close to the edge, blackness is creeping in at the sides of your vision. Soon you will be unconscious. You can barely hear yourself now, your first stoical grunts quickly turned to roars, but now all the sound that is left to you is automatic, each breath thumped out of you producing its own soft, chordal moan, as primal as a baby's sob.

The men stop, you can hear their laboured breathing; it has not been an easy task to fell you, a giant country oak full of knots and sap. "Alo, there's no call for this. We're not animals. Give us the keys." You can scarcely see, you can just about speak, "I don't think you're animals, you're doing what you think is right, it's in your nature." You gasp and drag another hacking breath into your burning lungs. "But I can't give you the tractor to plant your bomb. I just can't, it's not in *my* nature."

Number Three bends down and kneels on the concrete beside you, a priest's genuflection before the final benediction. In slow motion you see the handgun approach your left temple, lazily whipping you towards blessed oblivion.

You wake in the hospital bed. Cormac is on a plastic chair beside your locker, upon which rests an incongruous bunch of grapes. Your son's face, still innocent of the razor, lights up at your first moan. Has it worked? The deception? Is it complete and clean?

You wake again tomorrow, you swim in and out of daylight. *Hospital is wonderful* you think, until you notice the spiders. The spiders are coming from behind the wallpaper, from cracks in the lino on the floor of the South Tyrone Hospital. Black-and-orange hairy, they surge from the locker drawer and out of the half-eaten grapes. The spiders swarm over you, making you claw and tear at your skin. The nurses hold you down, they murmur in your ear, they hush your screaming. "No more morphine," you beg, "I'd sooner the pain than the spiders."

One day the polis come. They toss their hats, with RUC emblazoned, onto your bed; Nurse Josie tut-tuts and removes them. Cormac is to give his evidence in your presence, he has no other guardian. *He came home, he found you in the yard, he called the ambulance. That's it.* He has nothing to add. Neighbour men are taking care of the milking, he is feeding the calves. He is sharing a bed-room with Phelim McNeill. Mrs McNeill is a good cook, better than you. All is well. He looks to you for confirmation, you nod. "Good man yerself, son."

Now it's time for your statement. The Royal Ulster Constab-ulary man turns to a fresh page of his notebook, licks the nib of his biro pensively. At first he makes a few desultory notes, then pauses incredulous. "The bull? The bull? You're telling me the bull trampled you? D'you think I came down the fuckin' Bann River in a bubble, man dear? Someone beat the livin' shite out of you . . . pardon me, Ma'am . . ." He blushes and looks quickly at the nurse. "I've heard worse," she shrugs, "I used to be a midwife."

You struggle to speak more clearly; every fibre holding your spirit to your body burns with a fiery ache. "The bull. He turned on me. Quick as can be. It happens. I was lucky to drag meself back til the yard." You are coarsening your speech, acting the bumpkin. "He turned on me and the cows panicked. God alone knows how many trampled me. I'm a lucky man."

"You're a damn fool liar!" The officer's outraged face is puce; a vein throbs in the very centre of his forehead. "The tractor was in the middle of the shed, the doors near ripped off, the slurry tanker cowped on the floor. We found the keys in a ditch. Explain all that, I'd love ta hear it."

"I can't explain none of thon, officer, I dunno what I was doing. I daresay I'd lost a bit of blood, had I, Nurse? Mebbe I was trying to drive meself to hospital—"

"In a tractor? In a *tractor*, and a Ford Cortina in the yard, half-full tank? Do you think that because the uniform's green we're all cabbages? We'll be back—and you can think about obstructing the course of justice while you lie there." The door slams back on its hinges, shaking a fine, sparkly film of dust from the top of the lintel onto the shiny, peaked hats as the men stalk out.

Cormac looks at you like you are the second coming of Christ. "God, Da, that's amazing. You got back from the oak-tree field on your own? That's a-maz-ing. Fuckin' Rambo you are." He takes your hand and a tear falls down his cheek. Your son is a toddler again, standing at the side of your bed, roused weeping from sleep, by a dream of his Mammy in Heaven. You blink and come back to the present, with all its pain and its joy. You have survived, you are here with him, he need not know about, nor fear, the shadows of the men in the masks. Nothing else matters.

"Will we have ta kill the bull now, Da? Now that he's dangerous?"

Your fingers fall weakly from his hand, the joy of holding it outweighed by the pain.

"We won't be killing him, he's no more dangerous than he was last week, and no less. Animals are always dangerous, son. None of us can change what's in our nature."

The Accidental Wife

:::::

JOAN SWEPT the hair out of her eyes with a dusty hand and blew a little spurt of warm air over her face. Spring cleaning. Why the hell did she bother? No one would notice. Where was Gemma? Girls did precious little housework these days, although maybe that was not a bad thing. As a child, Joan had spent most of *her* free time helping her mother, Marion; no shirking, no complaining.

In their small home in Omagh's new council estate, jerry-built to replace the slums flattened in the post-war building boom, Marion had rinsed, wrung, and starched, smoothed and ironed. This, in addition to cleaning other people's houses, had kept starvation at bay. Marion had a fierce conviction that every one of her neighbours despised her, not for being born poor, as they had been, but for a worse sin, for becoming poor, for coming down in the world.

After school each day, Joan helped Marion slide the pristine, pressed, and lightly scented clothing back into large, calico garment bags; green for Mrs Lambert, blue for Mrs O'Connor, red for old Mr Johnson. Her mother's laundry and cleaning came from both sides of the otherwise strictly divided community. "Catholic or Protestant," Marion sighed, "makes no difference. Paying slave wages is the only thing they agree on." Joan laid the heavy garment bags with care across the bar of the rusty Triumph bicycle and pushed it slowly, cautiously, to the wealthier parts of town.

Astonishingly, for a charwoman, Marion had also taught piano—the tuner hard pressed, each September, to wind the creaking, ancient pegs of the instrument into some semblance of tunefulness, cottage pitch. "I dunno how much longer I'll be able to keep doing this, Missus," he muttered every year; "next year the wire's gonna snap for sure, probably tak' me eye out when it goes. Then where'll we be?" Marion would sniff and slap down the precious shillings on the piano lid. "We'll cross that bridge when we come to it, thank you, Mr Jackson."

She clung to the piano as if to a drowning child. It was more than a means of making a living, it was a talisman, a good-luck charm, a declaration that here, at least, in this one room of her threadbare home, there was culture and the possibility of beauty. Her red, water-swollen fingers picked across the keys occasion-ally, plucking out sorrowful, weeping tunes in F-sharp minor, *the devil's own key*, she called it. By November each year, the flood of new pupils would dwindle to a trickle, as those with talent moved on to more expensive, more qualified teachers, and those without, slowly accepted their music-less futures.

"Is the piano left over from before Daddy died?" Joan asked occasionally.

"Ask no questions, daughter dear, and I'll tell you no lies." Or more frequently: "For goodness sake child, will you give my head peace? Can't you see how busy I am?"

So the piano remained a mystery, like much else about their lives. Joan could not piece the stubbornly fragmented puzzle to-gether. Certainly, Marion seemed not to belong on the coun-cil estate, did not sound like the other girls' mothers. There was no roaring, no threatening, in her home. Her voice was care-fully modulated, alien among Omagh's broad vowels and coun-try thicknesses.

"Did you ever hear anything so coarse?" she would ask, *tsk-tsking*, as the neighbour women threw up their sashes to referee a dispute on the road.

"Cut that out, ya wee nyark, or I'll tan yer ass for you!"

"And you, Peggy Marley, you lay a finger on my chil' again and I'll throw you on the sheugh, ya bad wee cyarn!"

Joan would have loved to join the loud children of the street, the banging doors, the teeming, chaotic families. She carefully hid her longing from her mother—her secret wish for a quiet, long-suffering father, handing a few pennies from his pay packet each Friday to a host of younger sisters and brothers, bringing home a bar of Fry's Chocolate Cream to his noisy, raucous wife, in the hope of getting three shillings back, instead of half a crown.

"Lady Muck, here comes the daughter of oul' Lady Muck," the children on the street had called after Joan when they were all young enough to skip rope and push dollies. Soon they were teenagers, working in the linen factories, or shop girls, if they were presentable enough, and they maintained a hostile silence when they saw her, still in a school uniform, still bent under the heavy satchel while they smoked their Sweet Afton and went giggling to the movies arm in arm.

Joan had often stayed silent, watching the veins throb in her mother's wan, bleached throat as she bashed the stained clothing in the sink with such angry vigour that it seemed sure to tear this time. She was especially bad-tempered on Fridays. "Go down now, Joan, to Jimmy Marley's fish cart. Get two small pieces of ling, *small* mind, but not small enough to look like we can't stretch to a bit of fish on a Friday." Meat-free Friday was a real penance in their house, much worse than the meat-free Mondays, Tuesdays, Wednesdays, and Thursdays that preceded it most weeks.

: : : :

TWENTY-FIVE YEARS LATER, Joan had more than enough money, even if it took effort to prise it from her husband's wallet. She looked around the large, comfortable room she shared with Dominic. She pulled clean sheets onto her marriage bed, unstarched, unironed. Marion would have been horrified, but for Joan, good enough was good enough. She opened her mouth to call for Gemma's help, then closed it again. There were exams to be passed, lessons to learn. She would not stand in Gemma's way. "Please God, Gemma," she said often, "you'll pass from Queen's straight into St Mary's in Belfast, if you just buckle down to the books." Gemma would sigh, and pretend not to hear. "Teaching's the right job for a woman; respect, a pension, a clean job indoors with no heavy lifting. You count yourself lucky, Gemma, to have a chance at the teaching, like Auntie Nora."

Now that Joan needed help she did not call Gemma, she persevered alone. She did not call her sons either, Rory, Frank, or Jim. Their father had opinions on men doing women's work.

She had known all about Dominic's opinions before she married him. She had married young, and it was not a whim. She had known Dominic for years, had been to school with his sister Nora, had visited the farm many times and ridden the fat, grey pony with a rope tied to his head-collar in place of a bridle.

In the early years, she had been dimly aware of Dominic in the background, another nuisance of a boy, always ready to pull a pigtail, or to shove a girl into the brimming sheugh after heavy rain. A change had come, slowly, unnoticed between them.

"What're these steps for?" she asked, in the summer of her sixteenth year.

She and Nora were sunning themselves on the top of a short flight of concrete steps that led nowhere. It culminated in a flat, wide platform three feet off the ground. The girls had their legs angled carefully to the rays of the dying sun, skirts up over their knees. Not so long ago, the platform had been a pirate ship, a fairies' den, but those days were behind them now.

"Were they used as a mounting block?"

"How would I know?" said Nora, "They don't need sweeping, or dusting, they don't need peeling or cooking, I don't give a toss what they're for." She glanced around the yard and yelled, "Dominic, cm'ere a minute, answer us a question."

Joan tried surreptitiously to dust the worst of the horsehair off her ancient, shapeless skirt and puffed her fringe out of her eyes.

Dominic strode across the yard, long steps, countryman steps, and Joan felt a panicked tremble at the back of her throat, a lump rising up out of her chest. She turned her face, with a force of will, to Dominic's direction. He had shed his waistcoat; the fabric of his shirt strained against his collarbones as he carried a sack of grain with ease over his shoulder and walked quickly, his breathing calm, effortless. A wisp of black hair was visible, when he bent, at the open collar.

What age was he? He was older than Nora anyway—old, he must be twenty at least. He was the broadest man Joan had ever seen; his shoulders, massive from labour, bulged under the coarse fabric of his working shirt, and his body tapered down to a slim waist, long, strong legs. He was a grown-up man, just chatting with the school friend of his little sister, Joan silently reminded herself.

"This flight of steps, just sitting here in the corner of the yard, not going anywhere. What's it for? Is it a mounting block?"

"A mounting block?" Dominic laughed. "You'd know a lot about mounting, would you? I thought all you Convent girls had your minds on higher things than that. A mounting block in the middle of the yard? Sure the cows would run a mile if they seen the bull jumping at them like that. And he doesn't need a block, the size of him, he's five and a half feet to the shoulder."

"No," she explained, blushing and giggling while Nora snorted beside her. "A mounting block is a platform for you to stand on, to make it easier to get your foot into a horse's stirrup. It rises you up—handy if you're getting old or if your horse is huge."

She watched the humiliation rise across his cheeks. His blue eyes, dancing with summer laughter a moment ago, were as dark as a frozen pond under a grey winter's sky, and the lines around his mouth deepened. He was ugly in that moment, and frightening too. She didn't know much about men, but this much even *she* knew, they don't like looking stupid. She could almost hear the thoughts racing through his head: he was after making a big, country fool of himself in front of her—a little Convent girl from a little council semi with the inside bathroom and the immersion heater. He should have known she wouldn't be talking about cow sex, or any other type of sex either, for that matter.

"Christ Almighty, will you listen to Miss Enid Blyton, herself. It's a long way from mounting blocks *you* were reared, anyway." He seemed somehow taller, cold and hard as the stone steps. "Will you listen to Miss Council Estate. You'd know a fine lot about horses if it wasn't for our Nora here, whatever she sees in you. A mounting block? You and yer oul' posh Ma, playing pianos, all fur coat and no knickers. You haven't enough land to make a window box, never mind graze a horse."

He grabbed the sack of grain and heaved it over his shoulder as if he were heaving Joan herself, cursing as the rough sacking cut into the softer skin under his ear. He aimed a mighty kick at the loyal old collie who wrapped herself round his legs; the black and white bitch flew through the air, then limped, whining solicitously, after him, as he stormed off.

Joan sat silent; her face was blotched crimson, as if he had slapped her with his hands instead of with his words. Nora shook with laughter. "Jesus, Joan, that was funniest thing I've seen in months. It's not often a woman tells Dominic he's wrong. Don't you know he's God's gift to womankind? He wouldn't appreciate that from a wee lassie like you."

She hooted and held up her hand beseeching, "Come back tomorrow, Joan, it's hateful stuck out here on my own, sure we made great progress studying our French verb declensions, tell your mother. Tomorrow we'll try the algebra."

But it was weeks before Joan cycled out to the farmyard again.

Dominic's father had celebrated the imminent arrival of the 1960s with the purchase of a dull red, reconditioned Massey-Harris tractor. This year, with the arrival of the tractor, the hay had been made with minimum effort. There had been no team of neighbour men or hired labour in the fields. Nora and Joan had not been called upon to carry the huge teapots to the men in the meadows, nor to stand in the old kitchen peeling stone upon stone of potatoes for the haymakers' lunch. At any time, Mary-Ellen McCann was the quietest woman Joan had ever known. She scuttled round her big kitchen in silence, a mouse crossed with a bee, the quietest, busiest woman in Ireland. The old tyrant of a stove was kept alive day and night, fed with sticks and bark and precious, carefully hoarded lumps of coal, keeping the three ovens at different degrees of heat. This summer, without the huge teams of workmen to feed, Mary-Ellen seemed to have shrunk, to have fallen in upon herself, wasted.

Dominic's father, Tommy, chugged in the meadows, a cooling breeze lifting the damp hair from his brow as the haybob whizzed at dizzying speeds, creating uniform, even ranks of hay.

Joan helped out, as she had for years, paying for her pony-riding with the frail strength of her town-reared body. *Don't go riding Nora McCann's pony, Joan, unless you are prepared to pay for it. I scrub dirty collars and cuffs, for those who are well off but too mean to pay the laundries, so I never have a full slate of debt against me at the butcher or the grocer. Never a penny owed in this house.*

The coarse twine of the bales cut through her work gloves and reddened her palms as she and Nora, one to each twine, staggered, slipped, and somehow carried bales between them.

As she struggled to keep her side of the bale off the ground, she realised her eyes were straying, involuntary, unbidden, in Dominic's direction. They had not spoken since that day in the farmyard.

In time the trailer was full, stacked ten feet from the soil. "I'm not shedding off a single one of these bales on the side of the road, to be gathered by wastrels while we sweat," Tommy said. "Enough is enough, we'll do it slow and safe." Tommy swung into the driver's seat and the others clambered up onto the load.

Tommy set off, the tractor lurching and bucking, the overburdened engine groaning. As they passed through the gate, the whole trailer load swayed left, then heaved upright again. Joan clasped Dominic's forearm in terror, not entirely feigned. A bead of sweat escaped the rolled-up sleeve of Dominic's shirt, bringing with it a hint of armpit, of hair, and hard muscle. In wonder, Joan watched her fingernail trace the line it left on his arm, ending at the deep furrowed wrinkle of his wrist.

"Hey, Miss Blyton," he muttered, "no taking liberties there."

She blushed and withdrew her hand before Nora had a chance to cast suspicious eyes upon them.

"Do you know how heavy ten gallons of milk is?" he asked.

"What? No. Wait, eight pints in a gallon, twenty ounces in a pint . . ."

He laughed.

"I don't know either, thanks be to God, since we got the new milking machine. But my father did. And his father before him. You can't lift a ten-gallon milk can onto a cart, give yerself a hernia. You put the can on a height. Then you fill it, bucket by bucket, from the dairy. When the can's full you can just about swivel it over onto the back of the ass-cart."

He smiled and she saw that she was beautiful. This man was talking to her, in her yard clothes, last year's second-best. Her hair was stuck to her face and a moustache of sweat decorated her upper lip. And yet, here she was, beautiful, talking to a man.

"Mounting block . . . Sweet sufferin' divine. Mounting block, I ask you? What'll we do with you at all, Miss Blyton? Have we any chance at all of turning you into a farmer's wife? Away back to school with you and finish as fast as you can. Then we'll see."

Nora leaned over and shouted above the rattle of the engine.

"What are youse two whispering about?"

"Nothing," said Joan, "nothing at all, oul' rubbish."

Except . . . I'm engaged to be married. I think.

::::

SHE WAS INDEED engaged to be married. Nothing much was ever said between Dominic and Joan on the subject. It was established fact. Her friends laughed and joked; a strong, silent type, an Irish John Wayne. Not everyone was equally sanguine.

"Joan, love. It's better to be an old man's darling than a young man's slave." Her mother puffed in the heat of the kitchen and placed down the hot iron. "Are you sure you shouldn't wait a bit? Go to Belfast, get a job in a shop even, if you won't try for the secretarial course?"

Joan shook her head, silently. *What would you know about love, about anything?* she thought as her mother ran the steaming iron over a huge bundle of crisp, drying shirts. *There isn't so much as a photo of my father anywhere in the house. Out of sight, out of mind. We don't even buy a poppy like the Protestants do, for Remembrance Day. What would you know about love?*

She folded each hot, taut shirt as her mother handed it to her.

"It's done and dusted, Mother. He has asked and I have not said no."

"But have you said yes?" Hope sprang up in Marion's voice, deeply insulting. "It's not too late perhaps? A childish infatuation? A misunderstanding?"

"Mother, I hope you will come to our wedding. Whenever it is, I hope you will come?"

"Daughter dear, I will come to your wedding. There's no call for melodrama. I don't dislike Dominic McCann, I hardly know him. I just think you might wait a year or two, and work while you wait. Grow up a little."

"That's Mr Hutchison's load finished, I think Mother? I'll take them straight away, it looks like it might be turning to rain." Hoisting the heavy yellow bag over her shoulder, Joan closed the door on her mother's gentle remonstrations.

:::::

ON THE FARM, Dominic met stronger resistance.

"Joan Smith? Joan Smith? Have you lost your reason, Dominic? Joan Smith, to marry onto fifty-six acres? Are you out of your tiny mind? From the council estate?"

Dominic shrugged. "There's no such thing as a dowry these days, and I don't care where she's from. And there's no such thing as asking your father's permission, either. She suits me fine, and I'll have her, with you or agin you. I'm not asking you, I'm *telling* you. And I'm off now to tell Mrs Smith."

The door slammed behind him. Tommy McCann looked over at Mary Ellen, huddled beside the stove.

"This is your fault, woman. *Christian forgiveness, Tommy . . .*" He minced about, falsetto voice flaying the bowed head of the woman beside him. "*It's not the child's fault, Tommy. If she's good enough for the holy nuns, she's good enough for our Nora.* Well, tell me, woman," he roared, "is she good enough for our Dominic? And he's away off to talk to Lady Muck. *Mrs* Smith."

Tommy slammed his cup upon the stove, knocking a chip from the base that would serve, for years, as a reminder of this day.

"He's going to bring that wee bastard, that penniless by-blow onto my father's farm, to lord it over us with her town ways and her piano-playing? To smirk at a decent Christian woman, and run you out of your own kitchen, as fast as she can?"

He fixed his wife with a fierce stare. Then he played his trump card.

"I'll tell you something else. If Marion Smith is a cradle Catholic, I'll be damned. Changed over, turned her coat, I'll swear it, to avoid meeting any of her own type, who might know her from the old days. Might see her, with her little accident hanging off her apron strings. Now our Dominic's off to see *Mrs* Smith? I'll not see him ruin his life. I'm too long hesitating. I'll tell him the truth about Joan Smith th' night."

And he did.

::::

JOAN GLANCED around her bedroom, tucked the last careful fold of the eiderdown on the king-size divan that had replaced Tommy and Mary-Ellen's ancient, tight-sprung, iron bedstead, straightened up and sighed.

"Gemma," she roared down the stairs, in a manner that would have horrified her mother, "have you finished that history essay yet?"

Carphone, 1992

:::::

CALIFORNIAN DESERT scenery flashed past my windscreen. Sun-baked agaves and aloe vera shimmered in the slight, cooling breeze. Of all the things I love most about my job, my new life, and my adopted home, the weather ranks in the top three.

God! I'd been so right to leave Ireland. The unspeakable, dour misery of trudging into County Tyrone's sullen rain; head slumped low, scarcely visible between my shoulders. My father, walking ahead on the dung-spattered path behind the dairy cows; damp soaking through the shoulders of his jacket and dripping, chilly, inside his boots. Then the hostile, disappointed silence inside the milking parlour, punctuated with infrequent, weary complaints.

"Fuck sake Rory, are ye blind, can you not see she has mastitis? The whole fuckin' tank contaminated. Jesus Christ."

I might just possibly have survived as a farmer *here*, in this land of eternal sunshine, but at home, with that miserable bollocks gurnin' on at me? Never.

After I got the job, I bounded onto the plane, swaggering away from the parents at the security gate, no backward glance, no fake waving and mugging through the bulletproof glass at Departures. They didn't pretend to be unduly upset. My father lost three brothers to emigration in the days when they were lucky to get back once every ten years; I remember the Yanks coming "home" onto the farm the odd time, tossin' money round in McConville's pub, in their fancy clothes, causin' upset and resentment among their kin. My Da never pretended to miss *them* either. No, my parents were glad to be shot of me, really. I'd never cooperated, never fitted the mould of the oldest son, the heir, the farmer.

I don't let them forget me though. I never let three months elapse without fitting in a fleeting visit to Tyrone, on my way to London or Paris. I don't enter the shitty milking parlour, I sit in the kitchen, looking at my Rolex—they don't know it's a knock-off—eating tart and talking about money and sunshine.

::::

"GOD, THIS IS the life!"

I reached out and stroked the walnut dashboard of the speeding car. I was spinning out a sales trip round the rural hinterland of Los Angeles, showing brochures and scheduling demonstrations for likely purchasers of colossal, American industrial-farm machinery. Money was no object in these vast ranches, milking one thousand cows to my father's eighty. Normally, I flew between sales meetings. This month, however, I got my secretary to spend several terse days inventing an itinerary so I could justify hiring a luxury sedan and a week's driving.

"I wanna see a bit of the country, Rita, I wanna drive the back roads and take in the sights."

"In rural California? Our clients live in places like Fresno, you know? You know California's a shit-heap once you leave LA, right?"

"I wanna see Fresno properly for once, not just the airport. All them places. Why not?"

"Because they're full of sand? And hicks? And rednecks?"

"And women. Don't forget all those lovely, lovely women, Daisy Duke an' all her friends."

Rita snorted, shook her head, and picked up the phone to call Hertz. The economics of the trip just sneaked in under the radar of the company's expense-account rules.

:::

"WHAT A CAR! What a fuckin' machine!"

I'd never seen or driven anything like it before. A year ago, I walked out of LAX onto the airport concourse, and the heat was a physical assault that struck me like a rock in a sock. Prickles of sweat erupted in my armpits, and I dropped my backpack onto the pavement and panted like a busy dog at sheep-dipping time. I stood watching the airport taxis and black limos idling. I was always drawn to machinery—I was drivin' tractors at nine years old, standin' up so I could see over the steering wheel while still reaching the pedals. I hated seeing machinery suffer. I tapped nervously at the window of a limo and it purred open.

"Whaddya want?" The driver took one look at my rumpled clothes, my battered backpack. "Whaddya want, I'm waiting for someone."

"Erm, the car, erm, you know, it's got a leak. There's something dripping just under the engine."

"Are you for real?" The driver looked round anxiously, waiting for a scam. "Are you for fuckin' real? That's the air conditioning."

The window slid back up, and I was left staring at the distorted reflection of my red, mortified face before I turned away and trudged to the bus depot.

I couldn't live without air conditioning now, could hardly imagine being the hairy-back eegit who thought the limo was leaking.

But in this amazing hired sedan, I had a new toy. It rested invitingly in my right hand; as large as the sods of turf my Ma burnt in the huge, old stove at home. A complicated tangle of cables trailed back to a shoebox-sized apparatus nestled snugly between the front seats.

"A carphone! A fucking, honest-to-God carphone! God bless America."

I was Jim Crockett from *Miami Vice*. I wouldn't go home alone from the bar tonight. I still couldn't understand American girls, giving away for free what any man would happily pay for. Last night in Fresno, I just offered the best-looking girl in the bar a lift back to her place.

"An expense account, a carphone, and an Irish accent, that's all it takes," I'd thought, as I flung her long, tanned thighs over my shoulders. "By the end of the week, I'll be talking like Darby O'Gill and walking like John Wayne."

I grinned at myself in the rear-view mirror as I thought about picking up a random girl back home. It just wouldn't happen. Irish girls needed to know your name, your school, your sister's best friend's brother, all that shit. In twenty years at home, I never made it past a *court*—a snog and a fumble—what they call here *second base*. Casual, confident sex is an essentially American skill, and I sucked it up like an ice-cold beer. It's second on my list, between the weather and the money.

To hell with it. I *would* phone someone in Ireland. The cost would be astronomical, but it would be worth it. Just to mention, ever so casually, the phone and my hundred per cent, sure-fire, babe-magnet car. If Rita, back in LA, couldn't find some way to hide the cost of the call among the expenses, I'd just have to pay it myself. It'd be worth it.

A vision of the phone at home in the farmhouse hallway flashed across my mind. It's within earshot of every room downstairs and particularly close to my sexless, rigid, rosary-bead-worrying mother in the bustling kitchen. Doors swing open constantly into the hall; labourers, delivery men, bulk-milk-tank drivers, there's no privacy at all.

I wouldn't waste the extravagant call on my parents. I phoned weekly; Sunday was only three days to wait. I would call Eoghan or Vinnie. I quickly calculated the time difference. Eoghan was sure to go out later, propping up the bar at McConville's, embellishing the story to our mutual friends. Eoghan would be glad of my success, he would keep waffling and pretending that one day he would get off his ass and fly to California too. He would take a huge swallow from his pint of Smithwick's and discuss my opportunities for effortless sexual conquest, and Vinnie and Paddy would shake their heads and swear to one day be just like me.

I punched in the lengthy number. The connection took about five seconds. The ringtone was tinny and small in the receiver, but distinct.

"Pick up the phone, pick up the phone," I muttered until Eoghan answered. The guttural, bog-country accent grated on my ear. Eoghan sounded so coarse and dull compared to the bright, nasal Californians.

Did I ever sound like that? So gauche, so slow?

"Eoghan lad, how the hell are ya? It's Rory here. You're never going to believe where I'm calling from!"

"Jesus, Mary, and Joseph. Rory, it's good to hear your voice. Thanks for ringing." Thinking about it afterwards, that was a strange greeting. Eoghan's voice thickened further, blurred with some suppressed emotion. "Listen, boy. I'm *so* sorry to hear about your Ma. I saw her at Mass on Sunday. I just can't believe it."

I slammed my foot on the brake, swinging the car over to the dusty shoulder. Hot tears sprang up, taking me by surprise, behind my Aviator shades. It had happened. No, it could not have happened. My mother was only fifty-one years old, for God's sake.

I'd been on the road two days already, plucking up courage to use the shiny new phone. How long, and how desperately, had the family been trying to find me? How many calls had they fruitlessly placed to my apartment, the office, the pub? The funeral arrangements would be made already. Was everyone waiting for me? Why the hell had the office not tracked me down? Would they understand the speed of an Irish funeral, just three days after the death, and the essential nature of my presence at the wake in the farmhouse?

By now Auntie Nora would have decked the place out in white linen, carefully folded and draped. The clocks would have stopped. Neighbour men would be finding their way around the unfamiliar milking machine, things would go amiss, the cows always suffer from the ministration of strangers.

I was needed to shoulder the coffin, I would be *first lift*, with the Da and the two teenage brothers. Was it possible that a mother's death would not warrant a few days off work, in this career-obsessed society?

"Oh my God, Eoghan." I fought for breath, there was a weight on my chest, crushing, suffocating. "What happened? Is she really dead? Tell my Da, tell him I'll be straight home. I'll be home tomorrow."

Eoghan started to weep on the other end of the satellite connection—long, sobbing breaths—what the fuck? I'm the one should have been crying, right? Eventually he choked out some words, and I suddenly realised the little shit was roaring with laughter.

"Fuck sake, will y' catch yerself on, Rory. Who told you yer Ma was dead? I sure as hell didn't." He paused for dramatic effect.

"She's not dead, you feckin' eegit. She ran off last night with Paddy Buckley, from the accounts department at Maybrook Dairy. They've been at it for years, apparently. I wouldn't have thought she had it in her. Like mother, like son, I suppose."

The Ruination of McCaffrey

:::::

THE NEW-BUILT five-span hayshed loomed in the haggard, its freshly painted corrugated iron improbably green against the blue of the August sky. Square, golden hay bales filled two spans; the remainder of the shed gaped emptily, a mouth with too few teeth, a pointless, extravagant folly. Two spans had always been enough. The old shed, creaking in high winds, rusted slightly, had always been adequate, before this fool's errand of farm expansion.

The barn represented fifteen thousand pounds of someone else's money; repayments had barely started. The debt would live on long after McCaffrey was hoisted shoulder-high, then planted deep in the boneyard, two miles away. The church bells chimed their memento mori, mocking the iron structure in which a lifetime's plans and dreams had been finally buried.

Three days ago, the bales had lain in the already-greening meadows, a tonne of summer sun, joyous laughter, long bright evenings—and hope—encapsulated in each square bundle. Now they were simply fodder, nothing more or less, just dry grass to be mashed by the insatiable tongues and guts of bullocks destined to end up ground into patties between two toasted buns. The massive bales had been stacked in haste and with scant regard for safety, the top tier canted at a dangerous angle. So what? What possible difference did that make now? The worst had already happened.

The barn reared up out of the low-lying haggard, the tallest structure for miles around. The shed already had a nickname in the townland: *the metal mansion*. Soon it would become known as *McCaffrey's folly* or, perhaps, *the ruination of McCaffrey*. A gust of wind arose from nowhere and battered the building; it did not flinch or squeal. There was no loose nail or rivet anywhere in its wrought-iron skeleton to catch the draught and shift, howling or rattling. It had been built by craftsmen, masters of their trade, no expense had been spared. Big deal.

A taut ratchet rope thrummed in the wind. The stack was a makeshift, careless, throughother job of work. The toppling, unbalanced pile of bales should be undone, piece by painstaking piece, and restacked in a safe and careful way. Instead, the blue webbing of the ratchet rope encircled the top tier, secured to the stanchions of the barn, bulging and straining in its task of supporting the weight of nine or ten tonnes of hay, barely balanced, on a knife-edge. Even the loose end of the rope, cracking whip-like in the wind instead of carefully tied and threaded through loop after loop, revealed the lack of care with which the job had been undertaken.

Three boys had played in the old two-span shed in the days gone by. Now two remained, strait-jacketed in suit and tie for the evening's formality. McCaffrey had sent his oldest son to school, had not chained him to the pasture nor to the plough. He had not sent him off to Greenmount Agricultural College with the rest of the local gob-daw hairy-backs. McCaffrey had sent his son to the Faculty of Agriculture at University College Dublin, where the monthly rent on a tiny bedsit flat, with streams of damp coursing down the walls, would have paid for a little palace in Belfast. Yes, the University was where he had sent his boy, where a slim, hard-backed textbook might cost a hundred pounds. The boy was a year away from coming home for good, just one more September to June. *His* were the grand plans, his was the desire for the five-span shed. His voice had cracked and risen in pitch as he carried McCaffrey's vision on into the future: one hundred cows, a hundred and twenty, *more*, even.

Now, from the farmhouse window poured the sounds of tea-drinking, sandwich-eating neighbours—O'Neills, O'Donovans, McKeevers, McCanns—come to join in the Rosary. The coffin was closed. The boy, within, was a sight no mother needed to see. The hurtling bricks, the tumbling tiles, the shards of glass free-wheeling through the ghastly silence, before the sudden sonic boom of the bomb blitzing through Belfast's shopping centre, had ruined young McCaffrey.

Breathing

::::

"GET UP outta that, Alo! Get up and come with me now. The calf is dying."

A gust of wind ripped the farmhouse door from Gemma's hands and slammed it backwards on its complaining hinges.

"I think the vet might be heading the same way."

With a grunt, the old man levered himself out of his sagging armchair and hurried to join her. In the dairy they found the calf, stretched stiff on the concrete floor. Needles and syringes lay all around him while the vet, ghostly pale, rummaged in her bag, muttering to herself.

He was a decent-sized animal, eight months old, fattening for their own freezer. It was an old-fashioned practice for a modern dairy farm, and Gemma found the few bullocks a bit of a nuisance.

"I've never eaten shop-bought-beef in my life," Alo always answered her complaints, "and I don't intend to start now."

Today, the calf was due for castration and to have his budding horns removed. Five minutes ago, Gemma had been leaning casually against the wall, watching the vet slide a carefully measured dose of sedative into the bulging vein, the first step in this minor, routine job.

"Calm down, woman!" Alo roared over the vet's babble. "What are you doin' to get him back up on his feet?"

She had already given the animal adrenaline, twice as much as he should need.

"I haven't got a long enough needle to jab him straight into the heart."

"Can you do nothin' more for him?"

Alo dragged the young vet bodily out of his way and hunkered stiffly down beside the prone animal. It was no longer breathing, the tear-film already evaporating from the surfaces of its unblinking eyes. Alo reached into the worn leather holster he wore on his belt and pulled out his ancient pen knife. He used it fifty times a day around the farm. His black thumbnail flicked out an attachment. It was not really a blade, as far as Gemma could see, merely a long, sharp spike. She could not imagine its designated purpose.

The old man grasped the beast's muzzle, as any stockman will do, and regarded it for just a moment. He spoke quietly, but firmly, into the young bull's ear.

"Get up outta that, ya lazy bastard."

Abruptly, he rammed the length of the metal spike into the velvet-soft muzzle, splitting the septum, right up to the hilt of the knife. Gemma saw the vet flinch, as the last vestige of colour left her lips and cheeks; she readied herself to catch the young woman if she fell.

The bull's nostrils slammed open on the instant and he sucked in a huge, shuddering breath, rasping like a stone caught under a tight-fitting door.

"Good man yerself," Alo exulted.

He grabbed a towel and started massaging the rough coat—rubbing warmth and life back into the spastic limbs. He glanced up at the vet and spoke at last.

"Acupuncture."

"What?"

"Acupuncture point. Respiration centre."

The women picked up the litter, matching every discarded needle to its case, until they were satisfied that no sharps remained to injure a valuable cow later on. Then Gemma declared she was taking the shocked and shaking vet to the house for tea.

"And put a good splash of brandy in it," Alo ordered.

"Frig sake, Alo. You can't give people brandy at eleven in the morning with the cops round every corner. Sugar is what she needs."

Gemma half-led, half-pushed the vet into the warm farmhouse kitchen and wet the tea. When a little colour had returned to her cheeks, Alo came in and sat opposite her.

"What, in the name-a-God, did you do to cause the calf to keel over like that?"

The young woman started her defence, her voice rising in pitch uncontrollably. She had done nothing wrong, she had given the right dose, the right drug. She had done nothing wrong. She didn't know what to do. She had done what she could. She had done nothing wrong.

Alo reached across the table and took her chin in his huge, calloused grip. He turned her face gently towards his. The girl visibly winced. *She's afraid of him*, Gemma thought, *afraid of this crazy old man*.

"So tell us what-all you learned th' day then, lassie?" Alo's voice was quiet. She stared at him. She did not speak.

"I'll tell you, daughter dear. You've learned a clatter of important things th' day. I'll spell them out for you. Firstly, sometimes things go wrong for no bloody reason at all. Secondly, everyone has something to teach, no matter how old and crazy they look."

He smiled self-deprecatingly before finishing his long speech.

"And finally, you've learned that the most important thing in this life is to keep breathing. Breathing. You can call it pranayama if you want. Just breathin'. That's the biggest difference of all between livin' and dyin'."

He patted her hand and smiled.

"That business with the knife. That's a trick I saw used once, over sixty years ago, by Connors the bone-setter. It was long before there was a vet within cycling distance of this yard. I reckon it must be acupuncture, though old man Connors wouldn't even have known the word. I never hoped to have to do it myself."

The vet looked down at the table again. "I didn't know what to do, I thought he was dying."

"He *was* dying, pet, so what did I have to lose? Drink up your tea and give us your keys, I'll drive ye home."

She had salvaged enough dignity to drive herself home in the end, after a final look at her patient. The young bull was already staggering around drunkenly in a straw-bedded stall. The old man stayed to supervise its recovery while Gemma got on with the endless job of running a dairy farm.

:::::

Dusk fell over the yard. Gemma and Alo sat in the kitchen of his home. The evening milking had gone well and for once there were no small, outstanding jobs to do before the bedtime checks. Potatoes rattled and hissed, steaming on the hob. They waited for Cormac to come home. He was doing a bit of overtime at the fabricator's shed, where he now worked, since gratefully handing over the running of the farm to his wife. The overtime salved his pride somewhat; the absence of his half-hearted efforts on the land had scarcely been missed.

Gemma glanced over at her father-in-law. He had not mentioned the morning's events, nor would he. The episode was over for him. If she wished to discuss it, she must raise it herself.

"That was nice of you this morning," she ventured. "She thought you were going to eat her." Alo regarded her from under thick white eyebrows, composing his few words with care, as always. "Aye, well, there's plenty around here who would have . . ."

He sighed quietly and placed his warm, rough hand over hers where it lay on the table between them. He frowned a little before speaking.

"Gemma, you know I never had a chance to have a girl-child. But I tell you this. If I'd had a daughter of my own, I'd make fine sure and rightly that no grumpy aul' farmer would make her cry over a scrawny Friesian bull, not worth two hundred pounds."

That was all he was ever likely to say on the issue.

It was warm now in the kitchen; last year Gemma had replaced his old Electrolux cooker with an electric Aga, at vast expense. It ticked over day and night, heating the whole house and the water too. It was a marvel to Alo. His thoughts strayed to his wife Bid, stoking and cleaning their temperamental old coke-fired stove, coaxing fruitcakes and bread of extraordinary lightness out of it, muttering a persistent background of unheeded complaint.

"Why did I not buy her the bloody electric cooker she wanted?"

The Electrolux had been blue and white with an eye-level grill and two ovens. It was the height of modernity in 1970. It stood in McGreal's showroom and had been Bid's heart's desire and the cause of short, infrequent rows. *God's sake woman, do you think money grows on trees? Would we be cutting up the Farmers Journal and leaving yesterday's news inked on our backsides if I had the money for a brand-new electric cooker?*

He had ended up buying the bloody thing anyway, dashing tears from his eyes impatiently—to Patsy McGreal's horror—for *he* could make no headway with the demanding old stove. He had been too busy in those hard years after Bid's death to cajole and coax it, as she had done.

Gemma glanced, as so many times before, down the full length of the old pine table. It was a huge expanse of board—ten people could eat in comfort there. How long had it been since the big table was put to its proper use? She thought of Alo and the boy Cormac, sitting side by side, crammed together at one end, alone. Bid was dead this forty years past, horribly young. Ovarian cancer had ripped her from her home and her family in twelve short, shocking weeks.

Three decades later, gradually, hoping against almost-extinct hope, Alo had noticed a pattern to Cormac's increased outings.

"I say, I say lad, is there e'er a sniff of a woman on the scene?"

Cormac fobbed him off, good-naturedly. "Houl' yer wisht, Da. D'you want me to bring home some young one who'll turf you out onto the road when she can't bear the slurry-smell of me any longer, and we sell the farm to pay her divorce lawyer?"

Alo had waited and watched, praying that, in time, Cormac would bring him good news. His old friend Sean Power had come downstairs one Sunday morning and found a half-naked young woman in his kitchen.

"She was wearing one of Junior's shirts," Sean confided. "It was like a racing greyhound—just a few inches from the hare!"

The old men roared while Sean Junior stood, fit to kill them, at the back door of the eleven o'clock Mass. He tried unsuccessfully to hush them, like a blushing old nun. Despite this unorthodox beginning, Junior and Helen had gone on to marry, and had produced two male children in four years.

Alo had longed for the day he might find a bare-limbed intruder in his own kitchen. It had never happened, though. It would never have crossed Gemma's mind. He reckoned they had not had much of a sex life before their marriage. The house she had shared with two other young women had been twenty minutes from the farm, a massive distance for a dairy farmer. Alo could count on the fingers of his work-roughened hands the times when Cormac had pulled into the farmyard, in a cloud of smoke at seven in the morning, flustered, embarrassed, and cursing. "Quit yer gurnin' now, Da, I'm warning you. I'm here now, amn't I?"

Perhaps that very lack of sexual opportunity was part of the reason they had married so quickly. Alo's friends had nudged and winked. *Oh it'll be a fine baby, for sure. Ten pounds weight; conceived on the honeymoon and born three months early.* Unfortunately not.

In years to come, the big pine table would remain, to witness Cormac and Gemma holding hands in the silence of the kitchen. Eventually, the farm and the house would pass to someone who would discard the old table and replace it, and fill the house with a big, noisy family. She thought the new owners might even pull the old house down. It was damp and dark and had seen no improvements for decades.

She looked over at the gruff, weather-beaten face. Her heart swelled with sympathy and with gratitude. She could not have found a better man for the role. He knew about love and he knew about loss. He was an old man, twenty years older than her own mother, but he was also a dairy farmer with a pedigree herd. He knew all about fertility when Gemma and Cormac were just starting out on that journey. She could look him in the eye and use words like "cervix" and "flush" and "semen" and he would not blush or look away. He knew that some pairings were destined to failure, and that sometimes neither prayer, nor medicine, nor surgery would change that fact.

Alo was no stranger to infertility. His Aunt Mae had been barren, in the years when prayer was as much help to a woman as medicine. Alo had told Gemma of Mae's efforts. Fr Peter Deenan had helped to organise an expensive and lengthy pilgrimage to Lough Derg and to the Marian shrine in faraway Knock, Co Mayo. The journey through the Civil-War-torn country had taken a week by cart and bus, to no avail.

An even more complicated, illicit trip had taken place several years later to the Comeragh Mountains in Waterford. Mae had travelled the last leg of the exhausting journey, up the steep slopes of the mountain, on a small grey ass, marked with the sign of the cross on his withers, a reminder that one of his race had been good enough for Our Lord and Saviour and was surely good enough for Mae O'Donovan. Guided by an ancient, well-paid tinker-woman, devout, orthodox Mae had abjured her faith and hung a piece of rag on an ancient fairy tree. Its magical powers were well trusted by the gypsy women. Mae had sworn to bring a thanksgiving gift on her return trip next year, after the promised confinement to come.

Gemma wondered what complicated lie could have explained her absence for such a long time to the curious ears of Fr Deenan in the confessional. Poor Mae had not received her blessing, neither from the Christian nor from the pagan source. She had died an old woman, cared for by her nieces, in a way Gemma feared was probably a thing of the past.

She looked out across the yard at the mobile home where she and Cormac still spent their nights. Its small windows blinked back at her, accusingly.

"It's a temporary measure, just 'til the children outgrow the spare bedrooms," Cormac had said. "Then we'll build what we need."

"Jesus, that won't take long," Gemma snapped. "Get a cot and a playpen and a high chair in here, and we'll have to sleep on the roof."

Over the long, waiting years, they had come to spend more and more time in the farmhouse with Alo. The old man's un-concealed love for his only son, and his no-longer-young wife, permeated every corner. Love disguised the peeling wallpaper. It illuminated the Sacred Heart and the Papal Blessing from Paul VI, bestowed on Alo's own short marriage. Love transfigured Gemma's dismal surroundings. It enfolded and cemented her marriage. It protected them all from the sudden pangs of grief that struck unbidden, without warning.

She took his hand in hers and gently thumbed the ugly, purple warfarin blotches that poked out of his frayed cuff. He covered her hand with his other one; a stack of hands, work-hardened and short-nailed. Two large hands. Two small ones. They sat united and waited for the man they loved. Life could be a lot worse. They just had to keep on breathing.

Death Sentence

: : : : :

THE DOCTOR swept off his glasses with a practised gesture and folded them pedantically before speaking. Self-satisfaction oozed from his every pore.

"Mrs McCann, I have to agree with your research. The internet is a wonderful tool for preparing for a consultation. Often though, Dr Google is relied upon *too* heavily—you made the right choice coming to me today."

Prat.

He placed a cool, dry hand over Lucy's, lying palm up on the table. He administered a carefully judged pat before withdrawing.

Condescending, paternalistic twat.

"Mrs McCann. If, indeed, your husband does suffer from sleep apnoea, then yes, his life expectancy will be dramatically reduced. Every new clinical study adds further evidence to back up this assertion. Luckily for him, he has a caring, and careful, wife."

Lucy's heart pounded, not in her chest, somewhere up in her throat, choking. A prickle in her left armpit preceded a trickle of sweat, defying her expensive antiperspirant. Life without Jim. Unbelievable.

Jim had been her first real boyfriend. They had met at the Convent formal dance, tuxedos, tall shoes, talk of tractors. Jim was a lucky man, a second son, his oldest brother long since fled to America without a backward glance at his rightful inheritance.

Lucy's friends laughed at her sudden interest in agricultural matters.

Jim and Lucy had smiled at their stunned families; had scampered, vestal pure, up the aisle, neither of them twenty years old.

The doctor's voice was a faint drone, the whine of a bored mosquito.

"Every tiny incident, every stoppage and blockage, every moment of hypoxia . . ." Mr Lyons broke off. "That's a lack of oxygenated blood to the brain . . ."

"I know what hypoxia is." *You smug pillock.*

"Good girl. Anyway, this hypoxia causes infinitesimal damage to the blood vessels, the lungs, even the brain cells. Over the years it all adds up. Mr McCann should come in straight away to start the diagnosis. "

"Mr McCann doesn't believe there's anything wrong. He says he's tired because he works too hard . . ."

Fingers steepled, lips pursed, the doctor generously included her in a conspiratorial smile.

"But we know better, don't we? Get him in quick. Here's Sheila's number, tell her I said you're to have the first cancellation appointment. Strike while the iron's hot, don't you know?"

Lucy sagged a little in her chair. Jim would never walk willingly through the door of this hospital; he was a blood-shy dairy farmer, he shut his eyes, or called for Lucy, when the vet produced a scalpel, or blood arced and pulsed from a sawn-off horn.

:::::

THE TROUBLE with snoring is that, almost by definition, the snorer is beloved. Did Lucy care about the snoring of her mother-in-law? Only when some horrid twist of fate, some false economy, had left them sharing a bedroom at Cousin Emer's wedding. The snoring of one's husband is a different matter.

For fifteen years, Lucy had tossed and turned. Her heart hammered, her pulse raced. Insomnia was her constant companion. Periodically, the tortured rasping stopped. Silence. Silence. Five seconds. Ten. Twenty. Abdominal muscles strained and heaved until, with a gasp and "pop" that shook the mattress, Jim surged back to life; another close call, another lucky escape.

The dawn found them both awake, exhausted, pale.

The spare room was no longer an option. Lucy could not leave him alone at night. She could not enter their bedroom—chilly dawn, half-light—and find him cold.

After she had discovered obstructive sleep apnoea, Lucy became a dog with a bone. "You could die. At forty-five years old. I could wake up and find you dead. My life, my dreams. Go to the doctor."

"Jesus, woman, you have to change the record. Fifteen years I am listening to that one."

"A colleague of mine died from that," said her friend Clare, shaking her head over a large, skinny latte. "Young man, not fifty years old. Heavy smoker too, of course. Jim smokes a lot, doesn't he? Drew just never showed up to work one day. God, we were pissed off, we'd a massive rush order on. Three days later we were all standing in the rain, black umbrellas hindering the coffin bearers. Bloody awful day. We lost the contract too, even though we pulled an all-nighter to cover the hours wasted at the crematorium."

:::::

LUCY LEANED ACROSS the expanse of realistic oak veneer and stared Mr Lyons in the eye.

"How long?" she asked. "How long might it take off his life? Compared to smoking, say? Compared to diabetes? I need to know, I have to persuade him."

"If all my patients had a wife like you, Mrs McCann, my job would be a lot easier." He coughed self-deprecatingly. "We Irish men aren't the best at asking for help, are we?"

Answer the frigging question, you overpaid stuffed shirt!

Lucy smiled, a simper that she hated and despised, but that seemed to work on most men. "Oh, I'm sure you're not included in that statement, I'm sure *your* wife has no fears about your self-neglect. How long? On average? How long? I'm not asking for a date, just your best expert opinion."

Glasses back on and adjusted. Tie straightened. Large, mono-grammed handkerchief employed with a disgusting snottery sound. Stalling. Stalling.

"How long?"

A single, wayward tear defied her rapid blinking and slowly teetered over the centre eyelashes. It slipped discreetly down through her UV-defying, fatigue-disguising day cream.

::::

THE TROUBLE with snoring is that in time it becomes a third person in the marriage. Jim's snoring was the other woman, the indiscreet text message, the unfamiliar, female friend on his Facebook page.

"Jim works too hard and he snores?" her friends asked. "He falls asleep in the middle of the *Late Late Show*? Sure, who wouldn't?"

"He's too tired to go drinking with the lads or play golf at the weekend?" The coffee morning broke into hasty comparisons. "Give me your problems any day, Lucy."

"I'd rather have a prematurely middle-aged husband, snoring with the remote in his hand, than the flighty bollocks I'm stuck with . . . He's at it again, you know . . . I slipped his phone out of his pocket while he was showering." Attention fled from Lucy to Caroline. Loyal, steady, faithful Jim was never going to win the *Worst husband of the year* contest; not for snoring.

::::

"HOW LONG?" she asked the doctor again. "What kind of long-term impact are we talking about here?"

Abruptly, Mr Lyons gave in. He needed his rooms back. There were half a dozen other chequebooks in the waiting room already, the worried-well, flocking for the reassurance that the crowded, blood-smeared public hospitals never had time to provide. After a flurry of caveats he spoke.

"It could be as much as five years, I'm afraid, Mrs McCann. Truly, and honestly, it could knock five years off his life span, if he doesn't take the matter in hand."

He winced and tutted, hastily disguised as a cough, as a strangled whimper burst from Lucy.

"Five years? My God, my God. Five years."

Rising, she staggered from the room and thrust the chequebook at the startled receptionist. "Fill it in yourself, I've already signed it."

In the car park she fought for self-control. Head resting, uncomforted, on the hard, cold steering wheel.

"Five years. Five years. What fuckin' good is that? The bastard could live to be seventy-five. He'll see *me* out, if I don't get some sleep soon. Back to plan A. Pillow over the face. Not tonight— too suspicious. Soon."

The Quare Fella

::::::

"THANKS, JULIA, I'll take it from here. You get in touch with McDougal's and see if they're going to have that title search finished before hell freezes over."

Frank leaned back expansively and glanced out the window of the office. Four years in fuckin' law school to sit here doing fuckin' conveyancing. Conveyancing was for women, for part-timers, harassed mums, who clung onto two days a week in the office just to get out of the house. It did pay well, though. Paid for all the glamorous days of wasted grandstanding in the court-houses or in angry, bitter negotiations on the steps of the High Court. It would be great if McDougal's had fucked up, won-derful to blame this stymie, this stalemate, on another firm. If the title search was incomplete, he might as well head off to the club.

His secretary came back in, shaking her head.

"No way, Frank, it won't be here until Monday. I asked them about using a courier, but it's not ready and that's it."

"Useless bollocks." Frank didn't even bother pretending to be annoyed. "Look, I'm going to head off in that case. You give the client a buzz and tell them there's been a serious query raised over a Land Registry issue, but we'll sort it as soon as we can. I'm over there right now, in fact, fighting their corner . . ."

He winked and grabbed his car keys.

The road unwound before him as he sped from Belfast back towards the Gold Coast. Bangor wasn't so bad. He had resisted the move out of the city, but in the end had given in and now he lived in the sticks. What he had not banked on was the commute. An hour each way, sometimes longer, depending on the rush-hour traffic. Fantastic. Two guaranteed periods of tranquillity, five days a week. He never answered his phone in the car; it was *way too dangerous*. Springsteen was blasting, the sun was shining, and he was heading off early for nine holes of golf. Life didn't get much better.

"Not my bloody life, anyway," he muttered.

He deserved this chance to unwind after a long week at the office. The never-ending phone calls. The old biddies enquiring after their husbands' probate. How many ways are there to say *I need the bloody money* without being so crass as to mention the cash lying in the law firm's client account while the sexton and the gravestone carver become less and less polite with their enquiries about payment? Don't people realise that probate is the last thing on anyone's mind in a busy law firm? It's not a matter of life and death, that bit's all over. When a bank doesn't release funds for a client's mortgage on time—that's a crisis. That's the kind of thing people talk about, bad-mouthing the firm all over town. No one ever says, *Those bastards up at Jordan and McCann's have not organised my inheritance yet.* How could you say that in public?

Yes, golf was what was needed. Alice, his wife, understood golf. She understood networking. She knew that what a fella might leave unsaid on the fairway far outweighed anything he might write on a memo that could come back to haunt him.

Frank appreciated Alice—some parts of her, anyway. She took her role as the lawyer's wife seriously, maybe a little too much so. Her demands were few: huge sums of money, a good car, his pleasant, charming company in public whenever it was required. Luckily, Frank also loved dining out, Law Society dinners, Hunt balls. He had no objection to hopping into a tuxedo and allowing Alice to walk into the room on his arm. As long as they didn't end up fuckin' sitting together, with the ever-present risk that she would make a total tit of herself. He got enough of that at home. Let someone else try to follow her complicated, circular stories, confusing Neil Diamond with Neil Young, Botswana with Bolivia, her shrieks getting posher and faker with every glass of Bombay Sapphire.

No, all things considered, he didn't grudge Alice her showing-off nights out. They were a small price to pay to be left entirely alone the rest of the time.

Anyway, what had they to talk about? Most couples fought about money; but Frank and Alice need not. Most couples fought about the kids; Frank didn't worry about the kids. As long as the boys had tidy, short hair and Aoise had clean, white socks, that was the main thing, surely? It was Alice's department.

Most couples fought about their in-laws; Frank and Alice sidestepped that issue by avoiding their parents to the greatest extent possible. Yes, he had it good.

He folded out of the supple, champagne-leather car seat, straightened up and shook the hours of office stiffness away. Oh Christ, here came that insufferable bollocks, Paul Grayson. He had a hopeful, hungry look about him. No way was Frank sharing his tee box with that droning God-botherer. Teetotal, church-going, non-smoking Grayson must have some reason for paying his membership fee, but Frank couldn't guess it. Maybe he actually enjoyed the game?

"Grayson, my man, how're ya keeping? Great weather, oh yes, great for the old golf. But you wouldn't believe how little I play these days . . . oh the old handicap will be getting higher soon. I'm murder to go round with."

"Perhaps I could give you a few pointers? If we went out together? What do you say, will we pair up?"

"Oh God, I'm sorry, Paul." Frank deployed the smile that he reserved for female police officers if he was called to the station. "I can't. I'm in a four-ball already, with, erm, Connors and . . . erm, Billy Newel and one of Billy's lads."

A glance round the car park had revealed no sign of Newel's car. "I better wait for them, it's a longstanding arrangement."

Grayson sloped off.

"Good man, yourself," Frank muttered. "If I wanted self-improvement, I'd go home and watch opera on BBC4."

Next man to salute him was Diarmuid Carson, a man with a strange combination of names if there ever was one. Carson's father had been real old money, the kind of wealth where you married whomever the fuck you wanted, Taig or Orange, and to hell with the consequences. Diarmuid was just about tolerable. He was a faggot, unfortunately, but he didn't usually rub your face in it. In fact, Frank had had to be tipped off about that; Diarmuid could pass for normal anywhere—the money again, the old ability to be casual, that only the hereditarily wealthy knew.

"Now listen here, Diarmuid, if we see Paul Grayson out on the course, you and I have got together because I've been badly let down. Some mini-crisis in the Newels' extended family. Nice and vague."

"You're safe with me, McCann." Diarmuid trilled his plummy, upper-class chuckle. "Grayson won't be crossing our path, in case I give him AIDS or he turns queer. It's a communicable disease, you know. In fact, Grayson and his chums down at First Presbyterian could probably recommend someone to cure me."

Frank smiled and changed the subject. Jesus, it was one thing being cool and modern, and, of course, he was not prejudiced, but Jesus! It was hardly a topic for conversation.

Frank remembered a night in the early 1990s. He was approaching his A-level exams. He was heading off to University; third son, fourth child, he could choose his own future, as far as his father, Dominic, was concerned. The nine o'clock news was playing in the living room. Most nights the tales of misery and depression were barely noted, merely a prelude to the all-important weather forecast, beloved of farmers and of all those who worked outdoors.

"Shut up to fuck," Dominic would roar when the forecast came on. The room might be as silent as a Convent cemetery already, but the command came regardless, nightly, at twenty-nine minutes past nine. Tonight, however, there was no silence, no reticence during the news. Dominic was glued to the station, erupting occasionally in rage or wonder. "I should'a known. I should'a known all along. Only one types a' boys wears pink shirts."

Frank and Gemma were not even tempted to contradict or to criticise him. It was a unique event, by any reckoning. A prancing, dancing television celebrity was in the news that night. Simon Teesdale. He had been outed in salacious circumstances. Gay orgies, swimming pools, dead bodies! Frank was amazed that Dominic might ever have thought Teesdale straight. His father was near crying.

"I can't believe it. Simon Teesdale of all people." Dominic huddled closer to the screen. "I can't believe it. Name-a-God, Teesdale a shirt-lifter. A faggot. Unbelievable. He was a great wee entertainer, he'll be missed.'

"Daddy," Gemma had said, "he'll still be on the telly, he's not dead you know."

Frank thought Dominic was going to have a heart attack at his feet. "Not dead?" His face was flushed, an unpleasant beetroot-juice colour, the corded veins in his throat bulged. "Not dead? Well, he's dead to me."

::::

FRANK LOOKED UP at his golf partner.

"I've come a long way," he thought. "Can't imagine the Da swinging a club and chatting to a fuckin' fudge-packer like Carson. Swinging a lump hammer, more likely. Alice must be rubbing off on me. All that lovely old money. It's gone to my head. Surely, he'd be good for a few fees, if I could prise his work away from those old stiffs in Johnson and Lovelace."

Diarmuid whacked his ball bizarrely off course, sending it into the rough. "Goddamn it. What the hell was that?" Carson looked at his club in surprise, it was comical to behold.

"God, Carson," laughed Frank, "you're the quare fella."

In Plain View

::::

W*HAT THE FUCK is going on?* Lucy pulled her slime-coated hand back out of the washing machine. *Bloody kids!*

What the hell was it? It looked like frogspawn, but much, much smaller. Surely, they had not come home with pockets full of frogspawn? She was resigned to occasionally opening the washer door and finding three school uniforms liberally coated in flecks of Kleenex, or to discovering half a dozen pebbles clattering round at the base. But this was something new.

She pulled her devastated laundry out onto the spotless floor of the utility room. Everything was covered in gunk. She would have to rinse each piece by hand, rather than risk an expensive visit from the repair man. Finally, she discovered the root of her domestic disaster. Split open in the midst of the wet clothes lay the baby's disposable nappy. She had tossed it casually into the half-full laundry basket this morning, before dumping the contents, unheeded, into the thousand-pounds-worth of Miele washing machine.

"Fuck," she swore out loud in the silence of the almost empty house. "Fuck it to hell and back. Fuck and shit and crap and damn."

It was such a relief to let fly with her string of senseless vulgarity. She always kept such a tight rein on her language these days. Three teenage children and a one-year-old "surprise" will work wonders for the most hardened curser, she thought wryly. She had attempted, unsuccessfully, to address her husband's foul language too. Nearly ten years ago, Colette had asked her a startling question on the way to school. "Mummy?" she chirped, big blonde bunches of piggy-tails swaying, and her Dora the Explorer lunch box bouncing on her knee. "How come there are never any stupid fucking wankers taking up the whole fucking road when you drive me to school, but when Dad drives, they're everywhere?"

Jim had laughed 'til he almost vomited, and repeated it to all his friends, *and* to the family, who had found it highly amusing. Lucy had fumed, alone in her outrage. Luckily, the kids didn't see much of their father during the week.

In response to this incident, she had developed an impressive string of effective but non-lethal F-words. "It's all about the 'F' sound," her exorbitantly expensive parenting mentor had told her. "The 'F' sound, the labiodental fricative; any word will do." And it was true, up to a point. Her children were frequently subjected to a barrage of flips and frigs and even fiddlesticks.

Right now, however, alone in the kitchen, she felt entitled to some uncensored obscenity. She put on rubber gloves and scooped masses of tiny, hygroscopic balls of nappy-filling out of the machine and into the bin.

Forty minutes later she pulled off the sweaty, fusty gloves, reached into the huge American fridge, and cracked open an ice-cold can of Diet Coke. It was her first of the day; the first of many. She didn't drink tea or coffee—she was allowed one bad habit, surely? She looked over at the clock. It was almost eleven a.m. Soon the baby would wake from his nap, but at the moment, his monitor was silently reassuring.

I'm not addicted, she said in the accusing silence of her own mind. *Most of my friends would be on their third coffee of the day.*

Her Diet Coke drinking was an acknowledged fact, her one foible. She had at least one can each morning. She put one in her cupholder before every journey of more than ten minutes. She bought Diet Coke by the slab, twenty-four or forty-eight cans at a time, depending on the special offer of the week. She started to squirm if she had insufficient supplies to last until tomorrow.

If she drained her last can while Jim was delayed on his interminable farm work and the children were all in bed, she would itch and wriggle with the impossible choice of doing without or waking the children. When things were really bad, she would contemplate leaving them safely in their beds and driving to the village. *It would not take five minutes, all told. It was the same as popping into the shower for five minutes. Nothing would happen.*

All the ladies she took coffee with knew that she would arrive punctually at their homes, immaculately turned out, with a beautiful piece of home-baking, perfectly cooked. And they knew that while they ate it, drizzled with cream and accompanied by latte, espresso, or Americano in the hostess's best cups, Lucy would wash her portion down with Diet Coke, straight from the can.

"It has to be from the can," she patiently explained over and over. "It simply destroys it to pour it into a glass. I don't tell you how to drink your green tea. I don't care if you drink it out of a vase or a baby's bottle. I drink my Diet Coke out of the can."

In time, people stopped asking. It was a harmless enough eccentricity, even if it did look a bit uncouth. And, they all agreed, she was such a Marvellous Baker. And such a Wonderful Mother. And a Great Friend—always able to help out. *How does she cope?*

The can was half empty. Her dentist had warned her that if she must drink the stuff, it was best to drink it quickly. Her dentist was becoming her best friend, trying gamely to minimise the staining and the erosion caused by the massive intake of phosphoric acid. "Well, fiddlesticks to you too, Mr Dentist," she thought grimly.

Previously, dentists had always nagged-on about her smoking. As soon as she had seen the first blue line on her first pregnancy test, she had never smoked again; *well, one can't be seen in public smoking, with a bump, these days.* If she gave up her Diet Coke, they would find something else to nag her about.

The can was three-quarters empty. She looked at the clock again, twenty past eleven. Quick mental arithmetic—more than four hours to the first school run. Plenty of time. She was not a fool. More particularly she was not an addict. The important thing was to live one's life sensibly and to run no risks. That's what *addicts* do; they run risks. They lose control. They become selfish and careless. They put their children at risk. They hide things from their husbands. And she was not an addict. So she did none of these things.

She was a Loving Mother and a Supportive Spouse. She had many important roles to fulfil, and she was *absolutely thriving* in them. And she was not an addict.

Half-past eleven was still plenty of time. She took a large mouthful out of a fresh can. Then carefully, and with control, she measured exactly thirty-five ml of vodka into a measuring cup. With the ease of years of careful practice, she poured it into the can. She washed the measuring cup and restored it to its place (openly, for all the world to see) in the drinks cabinet. She replaced the premium-brand vodka there too. *She* had no secrets. She had nothing to hide.

She took a long draught from the opaque privacy of the can and felt a wash of calm rush over her. *If* she were hiding—she was hiding in plain view.

Waiting

:::::

A LO OPENED his eyes with a grunt. "Still alive then, I see," he thought. "That's good, that's good. Alive is better than dead!"

He ran the electric razor over the craggy skin of his cheeks. He was an old man, not a cripple; there was no excuse for slovenliness. Gemma had bought him the razor for Christmas. She worried that his shaking hands might slice into skin that thinned a little more each year, allowing the warfarin-damaged blood to well out. Gemma was rarely wrong about anything. His son had been a lucky man to meet her by chance, and to know his good luck when he found her.

Alo had worried long and hard about Cormac. It was a crime to see the young man sit by the TV each night with his father, watching Gay Byrne and reruns of *The Magnificent Seven*. Alo had been a great dancer and socialiser in his own youth. He knew that these days a strong, hard farmer with two hundred acres had no need to lie alone at night in a single bed in his father's home. Cormac was not shy. He was good company. He could sing (after a few jars), and Alo had seen him dance at many a neighbour's wedding. He was no more awkward on the dance floor than the rest of these young fellas, Alo thought.

Alo creaked his way downstairs into the kitchen. Wetting the tea, he glanced at Bid's photo on the windowsill. He gulped his cholesterol and warfarin tablets and washed them down with a huge draught of creamy unpasteurised milk, a slab of thickly buttered bread, and a smirk.

He said his daily prayer for the repose of Bid's soul, and added a relatively new one, for continued health and strength for himself.

"That's how you know you're getting old, Alo, boy." A young man does not pray for himself, he knows he will live forever. Alo grimaced. He was eighty-two years old, and he had no intention of giving up anytime soon. He had a reason to live and *would* live out of sheer stubbornness until he saw his dream fulfilled.

He was not ready to go. He clung tenaciously to his few, small chores. He thought of Bid, dead of cancer in her thirties with a child not four years old. Now that his own days were numbered, he thought again of her anguish. Leaving the boy. The daughters not yet conceived. The plans made, never to be consummated.

No, he was not ready to go.

Without wishing the man any harm, Alo planned to stand by Gemma's side when her own father was planted into the earth. He was twenty years Alo's junior, and had been dying for ten. Perhaps poor Dominic would welcome death and embrace a new life outside the shackle of his ruined body, but Alo would not. Besides, Alo had a goal, and that was something one could not say about Dominic.

: : : :

LEAVING THE HOUSE, he glanced over at the mobile home just twenty yards away. He had offered his newly married son his choice of any site on the land.

"I'll not leave, nor share, the farmhouse in which I was born. My parents and my wife died in this house. It'll see me out too."

He had been delighted with the young couple's prudence and thrift when they had opted for the mobile home. It was a temporary measure. "Just 'til the kids get too big," Cormac said, over and over to anyone who would listen. "We'll build a house when we know what we need."

"Good man, that's wise," Alo answered, "you don't want Gemma to build a castle, a bloody Southfork, like the McKeevers, then realise you can't pay for it. Likewise, you don't want to build something too small, end up with three dwellings on the farm instead of two, wasting a site. Or worse still, have to sell it, then have neighbours gurnin' every time you spread a bit of muck or mow a field on a Sunday."

Today, ten years later, his wispy, white brows knitted when he saw the mobile home. It must be a big impediment to the couple. What other problem could be standing in their way? The adoption people must surely object to the flimsy, temporary nature of their home. What other issue was there?

"It's madness," he burst out. "I've a right to put my foot down. If they will not move in with me, I will live out in the caravan."

It must be done soon. Cormac was no longer a young man. Alo suspected there was an age limit for adoption.

Gemma said the mobile was not a problem, that things took time. She said nothing more.

He had watched them devote five years to doctors and hospitals. His daughter-in-law had been poked, and prodded, and sampled, and half-starved. He had seen her cry in pain and vomit from the drugs. He had listened to her tales of medical indignities. He had held her. He had picked her up. Now she would not share this final part of the journey with him.

He ached to hold the child. He knew it might not be a baby. He was a realistic man. He was not expecting a pink and white bundle of newborn joy.

"Iggy Conlon has four grandchildren," Alo told Gemma, "three from Coalisland, one from Vietnam."

"She's a beautiful child," Iggy had said, "five years old and as black as the ace of spades." Iggy said there were many black children in Vietnam, reminders of the war, in need of homes and love.

"Jesus, Alo, you can't say things like that these days," Gemma scolded Alo when he told her and Cormac the story, but refused to be drawn on discussing her own prospects.

The old man sighed and went about his tasks. Gemma was in the milking parlour already; the machine's rhythmic suck and spurt echoed round the yard. Alo scratched the curly head of a fine heifer calf. She greedily emptied her bucket of milk, making a sound like a child with a straw in the dregs of a milkshake. How Alo would enjoy lavishing such childish treats on his granddaughter.

The adoption process surely could not take much longer, and he was a fine strong man for his age. He thought of all the love that the family of three had to share with their child, whenever she might come. Life could be a lot worse. He just had to keep on waiting.

Good Friends

::::::

A LICE WAS beyond bored. She looked around the sidelines
of the Rugby Club Juvenile Academy. *Honestly, there's no
one here, it's pointless.* She stamped her feet, frozen in their Ugg
boots. The damp grass was leaving a tidemark on the boots' soft
suede, she feared it might be permanent. *I might as well have worn
trainers, or a pair of fakes from Primark, for all that this crowd would
know or care.*

She inspected the throng of parents. Discreetly, from under
her tailored fringe, she viewed each face in turn. *Nobody, nobody,
nobody.* Her next glance rewarded her. That was Somebody. Definitely. Now she needed to work out who the woman was, and
how to organise their casual introduction. Maybe she was a television personality. Was it the presenter of *Nationwide*?

A roar went up from the small crowd around the pitch. Alice
craned her neck, feigning all the enthusiasm she could muster.
Clapping her numb hands together, she muttered to the person
beside her.

"Oh, well played! Who was it? I was a bit distracted for a moment."

"Well now, Alice. Do you not recognise your own son? Surely
you can't have been looking at the referee's six-pack by any
chance?"

"Oh God, yes, it was Iarfhlaith, of course, I couldn't see from my angle. Oh, he's mad about rugby. Don't you think he's showing a lot of promise? For a beginner?"

Really, she was going to have to learn the rules of the damn game. She never had a clue what the children were saying on the way home from their matches and training sessions. Most awkward of all was delivering her passengers to their waiting mothers, struggling to cobble together some semblance of a narrative on the morning's events.

She had hoped that by making her Volvo XC90 the unofficial club bus, she would become invaluable to these women. She had daydreamed of coffee mornings and race meetings and girls' nights out. Instead, more often than not, they simply replied that if she was sure it wasn't inconvenient, and if she was sure she didn't mind. . . . They hopped back into their own cars and scarpered.

Alice *did* know the rules of Gaelic football, and hurling. But that was even worse. She had already wasted two miserable, freezing years at the GAA Juvenile Academy, to no avail. There was simply no one worth meeting there. The parents were friendly enough, but they had no style, no get-up-and-go. Alice had decided it was time to quit. Iarfhlaith had been already resigned to leaving. He added Gaelic football to the lengthening list of activities sampled and abandoned: piano, modern dance, speech-and-drama. He was keen on athletics and every September he raised the issue again, but his mother would have other plans.

"The athletic club is rubbish. The track's lousy and the facilities dirt-poor. There's not even a clubhouse, just an old storage container and a few portaloos."

Iarfhlaith couldn't understand her objections; he didn't spend any time in the clubhouses.

Alice looked towards the field again. Her sons, Iarfhlaith and Ultan, were buried deep in a mass of struggling bodies. There was a ball somewhere in the melee. She didn't feel it was worth getting *too* au fait with the rules, because apparently they kept changing as the children got older and more physical. Her extent of understanding was that a ruck occurred when everyone fell upon each other by design, whereas in a maul it was by accident. Undoubtedly, there was more to it than that. A line-out was self-explanatory. "Kick to touch" was an expression radio reporters used to describe Government dithering, but had obviously originated in some mysterious manoeuvre on the rugby field.

A tug at the hem of her short Barbour jacket announced the arrival of her daughter, from the nursery group on pitch two. *Thank God. Twelve o'clock at last.*

Little Aoise was pinched and raw. Honestly, why choose winter to play the game? At least the GAA had the sense to curtail children's activities at Hallowe'en. Bundling the child into a warm Puffa, she tousled her daughter's hair. She loved all her children equally, *of course*, but with Aoise there was the anticipated added bonus of long, satisfying trips to Belfast and Dublin in years to come, maybe New York. They would go to Brown Thomas and Harvey Nick's. The boys, however, would happily leave the house wearing two refuse sacks tied at the waist with string. Her husband constantly complained about the children's designer gear.

"Jesus, Alice, it'll fit her for about six weeks, it's a total waste of money."

"Don't be such a miserable git, there are no pockets in a shroud."

She had even taken the trouble to look up "shroud" in the dictionary, to make sure she had understood her friend's expression correctly. She allowed herself a moment's brief disloyalty, sitting with the large book in her hand. After all, what woman has *not* occasionally wondered how much more peaceful and prosperous her life might be after sorrowfully redeeming her husband's life insurance policies?

Frank was a boor. He was a boor, and a bore, and a boar—she had looked up each word, she knew the difference. He enjoyed crushing her enthusiasm and reining in her more exuberant plans. She had got her own way with the children's names, however. Alice and Frank, she mused, Frank and Alice. Instantly forgettable. All her life she had resented her name. Alice. How she had longed for an elaborate, Irish name. She had never once been asked to spell her name, nor to explain its ancient Celtic symbolism to an interested American visitor. She had a list of prospective names for her unborn, even unconceived, children: Aoileann, Iseult, Manchan, Fachtna.

Her husband had countered with his own list: Sneachta, Uachtar Reoite, Dún an Doras. Eventually they had reached three compromises: "Jesus Christ, Alice, I'm past caring. Call the poor child *Earfluff* if you really want to, he can always change it when he's old enough."

The final whistle blew. The children clapped and leaped as their coach roared out some tawdry, inspirational rubbish about the best club in Ireland. Alice packed her own three kids, and three others, into the Volvo and pulled slowly out of the car park—really the spaces were far too small these days. Listening to the childish chatter with half an ear, she thought of the three good friends to whom she would now call.

She would go to Rachel last. Rachel was the cream of the crop. Her home was immaculate—she had only one child, Alice reminded herself. Rachel served her guests their choice of half a dozen teas, each woman presented with her own beautiful, tiny pot. When Rachel gave Alice a prawn sandwich or a plate of tiny samosas, a small sprig of parsley rested on top, freshly cut out of a flourishing windowsill garden.

Yes, she would go to Rachel last. She might be invited in.

Frank didn't like Rachel; *that silly pretentious bitch*. Alice and Frank rarely fought (or even spoke), but they had once had a massive argument when Alice returned from Belfast, laden with carefully wrapped parcels, and had produced six delicate Wedgwood teapots. Frank had ordered her to return them. Telling her what to do, in her own home.

"Fuck sake, Alice, you're so obvious. Everyone will know immediately that you're aping that rich bitch Rachel. D'you have to confirm what everyone already knows? You're a snob and a social climber."

"A snob?" Alice snarled. "Don't be bloody ridiculous; I barely have time to leave the house. Three children; no cleaner, no au pair. Who do you think is rearing the bloody children anyway? Social services would have taken them off *you* years ago—a scratch golfer who won't even bring his own sons to Royal Portrush."

"Alice, for fuck's sake, bring back the bloody teapots, or sell them on eBay or smash the fuckin' things. Just don't let anybody I know see you using them. Imagine handing my parents their own china teapot. You, who haven't done a day's work in your life, acting the society lady."

"Your parents! Dominic drinks through a straw, sideways out of a sippy-cup, though you might have missed that, seeing as he hasn't set eyes on you since last Christmas Eve. As for your mother, she's in some position to tell me how to behave."

:::::

SHE STROKED the tennis bracelet on her left wrist. It was not quite as heavy as might be expected after such a screaming match, and the silent, hostile week that had followed, but it was nice enough. She had spent a happy hour in Appleby's choosing her bracelet, though it would have been more satisfying had Frank come with her, to hear her discuss diamond colour and clarity knowledgably with the attentive sales assistant.

She pulled into the driveway of Susan's house first. Sue was a strange girl. Really, Alice might have to find a way out of this relationship. She gave you builder's tea, *strong enough to trot a mouse across* (revolting expression), in whichever thick-rimmed receptacle came to hand. She even used gaudy beakers which had contained Easter eggs in years gone by. Sometimes she rinsed the beaker out in cold water before filling it and handing it over. No sign of actually washing it. Alice usually dropped Sue's son off first.

She had once heard Sue say that she agreed with Professor Henry Higgins: the essence of good manners is not *how* you treat people, but that you must treat everyone exactly the same. Alice didn't know who Professor Higgins was—he was never on the radio, not like the gorgeous economics professor, Constantin Gurdgiev—but she wholeheartedly disagreed with him.

If only Sue weren't so nice. She listened attentively and never interrupted. She could be trusted not to reveal an indiscreet disclosure, or a moment of unguarded vulgarity. She was thoughtful. She was the type to turn up at your door with a casserole when your dog died, or your mother was ill. Unfortunately, Alice had had to throw the casserole away—the dish was chipped and harbouring God knows what germs—but, still, it was a kind gesture. No one else had come. She might hold on to Sue for a little longer, out of charity.

"Oh thanks, pet, I'd love to come in, but I've a whole carful today. Maybe during the week? I'll call you. Byeee."

She inched the massive Volvo backwards out of Sue's small gateway and on towards Maria. Alice wasn't sure about Maria. She was not particularly friendly anymore. She never invited Alice in for coffee. She was scrupulous about returning favours. She would insist on allowing Alice to return early from rugby training next week, as soon as Aoise's junior group was finished. Then Maria would pull into Alice's road later on, Iarfhlaith and Ultan crammed into her little Nissan, her own son on a booster seat in the front. She never called it a favour. She called it a rota.

It's difficult to cultivate a friendship with someone who never allows themselves to be under an obligation. *That's a good sentence, I must try to remember that.*

Maria used to be friendlier. During their first weeks at the Rugby Academy, she had been quite chatty. Once she mentioned that she sang in Bangor Chamber Choir. Alice had jumped at the opportunity. "I *love* music, I'd *adore* singing in the chamber choir. When are the rehearsals? I'm not a *great* singer, but more than good enough for a choir!"

Maria winced, almost imperceptibly. "It's just, you know, the music can be difficult, complex. Come to St Joseph's to meet Father Dennis. He runs the choir. He has a real passion for music, totally obsessive about Monteverdi and Vivaldi."

"Vivaldi? That's the English guy with the spiky black hair? Used to be never off the TV? I saw him once—he had a huge, great boil on his neck. Every time the camera did a close-up, you could see the boil bobbing along to the music, so close to the violin, I thought it was going to burst. Honestly, it made me feel really sick."

"What the hell?" Maria was looking at her in a very odd fashion, eyes narrow, lips quivering. "What are you on about? Oh, my God, do you mean Nigel Kennedy? Vivaldi's been dead these three hundred years. You know? It's a chamber choir? Chamber music? *Gloria in excelsis Deo*?"

"Chamber music? A choir that sings chamber music? Oh, I don't think I'd be interested in that. I thought you meant the choir of Bangor Chamber of Commerce."

For some reason, Maria had maintained a little distance after that.

Oh well, last drop-off now. As hoped, Rachel was free, and invited everyone in.

It was always a little difficult to control Alice's three muddy children in Rachel's pristine home, that fuckin' white box of a modern art gallery, as Frank called it. When Aoise accidentally wiped her jam doughnut down Rachel's raw-oak doorframe, Alice decided it was time to leave.

"Don't worry," said Rachel, face red and sulky. "It's great to have the house full of happy, noisy kids for a change."

While speaking, she was delicately dabbing at the doorframe with a lint-free cloth soaked in white spirits. A little hissing sound escaped her lips as she straightened up, inspected her work, and glanced at Aoise.

Promising a longer chat and a good catch-up someday next week, Rachel waved goodbye and closed the front door firmly.

Alice drove away, turning over, and savouring, the few snippets of news they had managed to exchange, between the irritating, child-related distractions.

What a bitch. I'm glad she doesn't talk about me like that.

A Wee Cup a Tea

:::::

"WEE CUP a tea, Daminic?"

Dilys bustled about, throwing open the curtains and cracking the window, allowing a tiny, tentative draught to disturb the stifling, still air of the room.

"Wee cup a tea? That's another lovely day, thank goodness, Daminic, although you farmers are never happy. Next you'll be wanting the drap a rain?"

"For Christ's sake, woman, get out of my sight. Do I have to listen to this oul' rubbish every day?"

"Good man yerself, just lift up a wee bit for me. Whoopsydaisy. Get that pillow under your oxter there. Now you're sorted."

"Name-a-God, there's no need to roar in my ear like that. I'm right here. No one ever said I was deaf, did they?"

Dilys mixed some thickener into a cup of lukewarm tea and carefully held it to Dominic's mouth at a precarious angle.

"Get that into ya, now love, plenty a sugar, just the way you like it. We'll get you ready early. I'm sure you'll have some visitors today, after chapel. Sure you're the lucky man with so many visits, such a dedicated daughter. Never short of a wee chat or a visit."

"The word is *church*, woman. I swear to God, they send you in here on purpose to drive me distracted. Get your wee Orange hands off me. Where's Mary or Aileen, even one of them wee Filipino girls, at least they're Catholics. *Chapel.* Don't make me sick."

Dominic gazed in impotent fury around the bright, airy room. Only the heat and the faint whiff of disinfectant from the en-suite bathroom marked the room out as a nursing facility. Otherwise, it might have been a mid-range, mid-budget hotel room, one in a long, faceless chain, competently managed. In other rooms there were hoists, lifts, even commodes, but Dominic had not plumbed those depths yet.

His bastards of children had him locked up here, incarcerated. What else would you expect from the spawn of that bitch he had married? On his chest of drawers there was a conspicuous, tidy absence. Other residents had trinkets and shrines in their rooms: children, grandchildren, wedding snaps, First Communion. Dominic had been strong enough during his first week to drag himself to the drawers unaided. Each framed photo had crashed through his unsteady fingers, until the floor was littered in glass.

Daminic, goodness sakes alive, man! And you in yer slippers! You'll be cut til bits. Don't move, man-dear, I'll have that cleared up in no time. You poor crather, what a terrible thing til happen.

Dilys and Maureen had carefully swept and mopped the devastated floor. Diligently, they preserved each flimsy rectangle of glossy paper, each technicolour reminder of that shower of bastards who had hidden him away here. Gemma had thanked the women profusely for their attention to detail and then had had the good sense to remove the photos. His chest of drawers stood ever since as bare and clean as in a room awaiting its next occupant, the family photos of old Mary, John, or Peggy waiting in a stout cardboard box for the day that their executor would come to settle the outstanding account.

"That's a great fella, Daminic, now a wee bit a porridge. Nathin' like the porridge for setting you up for the day. Whoops . . ."

Dominic remembered his wife at the same trick forty years ago, chasing errant drops of porridge around his children's faces with a soft plastic spoon, scraping it carefully off the pouting, dribbling lips and re-presenting it proudly, like a feast of manna and nectar mixed, back to the gaping mouth that had rejected it once already. He would like to spit it out too, as a protest, but it was the only meal of the day that resembled normal food. It was no worse than the porridge he had wolfed down as a child. It was a damn sight better than pureed stew or custard, which seemed to be his other staples now.

He should not have allowed himself to think of Joan, not even momentarily. He had not imagined his mood could worsen but, in the instant, a thick, black cloak of raging resentment shook its bitter raindrops over him before draping itself, damp and clinging, across his warped body, like the greatcoat he had always tied with baler twine to slough off the worst excesses of Ireland's farming weather.

"That bitch, that tramp. That mother of three sons-a-bitches."

"Now Daminic, love, don't talk while I'm feeding you, it's so difficult, and I know you don't want to make life difficult, pet."

"Oh, shut yer bake, woman. Get your wee Presbyterian face away outta my sight."

:::: ::::

DOMINIC'S FATHER had done his best to prevent the marriage.

"Catch yerself on, Dominic, I'm telling you. It's like the animals; what's in the bitch comes through in the pup. Don't hang yourself with thon penniless, wee bastard. Her mother hiding away out here in Omagh. In Omagh, for the love of God. What would bring her out west only her shame? Anyone can go into a jeweller's shop and buy a gold ring. It doesn't mean you're the loving widow of an army man, killed in Germany. Where's the army pension? That's what I'd like to know."

Dominic had flung his father's restraining hand from his shoulder. Old Tommy McCann never came closer to a punch in the face.

"If there's any shame here, it's nothing to do with Joan. It's the 1960s, Da. The world has changed since you took a bride. Marion Smith's not the only woman in the world ever made a mistake or carried on with the wrong man. If she did. And who in God's name is going to ask her? I've got no one's word for this but yours."

"Well son, you'll find the truth of it soon enough, when Fr McAtamney asks her daughter for her birth certificate. Bad blood comes out in the end; you're mad to take thon wee bastard."

::::

DOMINIC SIGHED and turned his face away from Dilys's questing, probing spoon. His Da had been proved right in the long run. Bad blood *did* out in the end. He had often seen it in the herd and his friends spoke of it too, at the mart and the abattoir. Many times he had seen how a bad bitch of a cow would breed nyarky, kicking heifers. A high-strung bull was not worth a damn— siring evil witches of cows, no amount of good milk making up for the difficulty with which it was coaxed from them. In time, Dominic had come to see that it was wiser, easier, and safer to sell these twisted animals and rid the herd of them. He should have rid himself of Joan.

"Dominic, lad," his uncle Peadar had said in the yard, days before the wedding. "If you'll take an old-fashioned piece of good advice? In the car on the way back from the wedding breakfast? A wee slap. Not hard, mind lad, don't mark her. Just a wee message that she's a married woman now."

Tommy had snorted.

"Bloody fool that you are, Peadar, if he wanted marriage advice from a bachelor, there's plenty going free up at the Parochial House. I've heard you talk a lot of shite in my day, but that's the height of it."

He turned to Dominic and raised a forefinger slowly, deliberately, a gesture of great solemnity.

"Only a fool hits his wife. Only a teetotal moron. Dominic, there's no call ever to lay a hand on your woman. Just find out how she thinks, then give it a little twist. Let her beat *herself*. And God knows she has enough to beat herself with, snaring a catch like you, and fifty-six acres with it. And her penniless. From the council estate."

Tommy paused and glanced over through the window at his wife, standing as always beside the stove. Her head was bent as though in silent reflection or in desperate prayer.

"I never lifted a hand to your mother, this thirty years, and I won't yet."

"Bully for you, Da, you're a model husband. I'm sure Mary Ellen O'Neill gives thanks to God every day for marrying the fuckin' pinnacle of perfection that is Tommy McCann. Keep your fuckin' advice to yourselves, or we'll end up at a funeral instead of a wedding."

He stormed across the yard, pretending not to hear Tommy roar after him.

"We might be as well off with a funeral, ya stubborn cyarn. Oh, you can be neither led nor driven, but you'll learn, in time."

He had learned, in time.

Slowly, during the early years of the marriage, he had acquired a few acres here, a few there. There was an out-farm, a piece on conacre, a derelict cottage five miles from the yard. By the time they brought his scornful, sneering father to the boneyard and planted him, and Dominic brought Joan into the big, cold farmhouse, he had seventy acres all told.

"Not bad for a start, Joan lass, not a bad start."

Old Mary Ellen kept to her room, more or less, she seemed quite happy to hand over the reins of the house and ate humbly and gratefully whatever Joan provided. To Dominic's astonishment, his mother began to blossom. Within a year, she was occasionally to be seen playing and frolicking with her grandchildren in a manner Dominic did not remember from his own childhood. He did not grudge his mother her late-found joy, he and Joan had enough to share. Seventy acres and two fine sons, they were on the road to happiness.

: : : :

"I'M HEADIN' OFF now next door, Daminic. You just ring yer bell if you need anything, love. Though I know you won't, niver an easier man was minded in this ward, that's what I always say about you."

"Thanks be to Christ, leaving at last. Close the door after you, you throughother hallion, leaving me here, half-fed, half-cleaned. Whatever they're paying you, it's too much, Dilys Wilkinson."

Dilys left the door gaping and bustled off to room 109.

Dilys was Dominic's number one enemy. He had always had one, fodder for his rage and spleen. The best days of his life had ended with his father's death. No longer united in their mutual repulsion against Tommy, Dominic and Joan had gradually come to accept that no fresh love had welled up to fill that vacuum of lost loathing. It was gradual, imperceptible. Before Tommy died, they had longed for his death, for their freedom from his sneering resentment, the solution to all their prayers, the root of all their problems. Slowly they had begun to wonder whether their problems stemmed from within.

Dominic could not remember how and when Joan's nickname had mutated. Living in a small rented bungalow, five minutes' drive from the yard, her ignorance of farming matters had seemed sweet, refreshing. Miss Enid Blyton he called her, with a slap on the rump after her many malapropisms, her misunderstandings. Miss Enid Blyton would laugh at him, untying her apron, eyes dancing; they would end up in bed, or on the sofa, with the baby gazing solemnly from the playpen. They were a modern, young couple; they had no need of darkened rooms, curtains, or nightgowns.

Once they moved onto the farm, however, her ignorance seemed insulting, confusing, disinterested really. How long could it take to learn the simplest things, how often could one woman make the same mistake? Surely her lack of progress was born of contempt?

"Christ, woman, all you have to do is wave your stick. Just wave your stick at the bull, drive him *this* way and the heifers will go the other way. It's not rocket science."

"Jesus, Dominic, you're *behind* the calves, all I can see is heads rushing at me, how would I know a bull calf from a heifer if I can't see between their legs? I'm not a mind reader."

"Are ya not? I sometimes wonder if you *can* read my mind, then do the exact fuckin' opposite out of spite. No other explanation how someone can get it wrong *every single* time. Have you any idea how long it will take us to gather those calves back up?"

"Us? Us? Maybe you'd like to try it on your own?"

Old Mary Ellen hobbled across the yard.

"Joan, love, go back into the kitchen with the babies. I'll do this. You shouldn't be upsetting yourself in your condition." She glared at her son, but risked no words.

One day, who knows why, who knows when, he had first snarled at her: Miss Semi-detached. She did not laugh with him. Her cheeks flared red and she rose from the table, then retreated to the safety of the sink. They did not require the creaking, cracking length of the sofa that day.

Years later the four children were well-up and nearly raised. That bastard Rory had already fled to California without a backward glance at his rightful inheritance. Now Jim was for the farm, Gemma for the University, Frank docile and quiet under the yoke of teenage acne. Dominic realised how much he had already given and how unwilling he was to continue. Joan had seen things differently.

"You're not the only man in Ireland, Dominic McCann. I could have had my choice."

"Jesus, who'd have you? Any man that could knock a tune out of you these days, I'd take my fuckin' hat off to him."

She had slammed out of the kitchen, so hard that the black-and-white Sacred Heart had bounced right off the nail and shattered on the tiled floor. "Well, that won't be goin' back up on the wall," she said later as she swept up the broken glass. "Creepy bloody yoke, it's only there 'cause your aunt Mary gave it as a wedding present. I should have taken it down on the day of her funeral."

"At least I had an aunt to give a present. It's a long way from turnin' up your nose at gifts *you* were reared. It's never enough. Never enough. Always a hand out asking for cash, for the car keys, for diesel, for school trips. What did I do to be cursed with this ungrateful shower of bastards? Hardly surprising, when you marry a bastard that she'll breed more."

"If you brought yourself in off the land a bit more often, if your children knew who you were and heard more out of you than roaring, you might like them a bit better. No—work and the farm are your religion. Hardly surprising, when a man is a shit, that he might breed another. You're cut out of your father, I might as well be married to Tommy, and didn't your mother deserve a medal for putting up with him?"

"Well, you'll be getting no bloody medal that's for sure. The land is my religion? Well, what would you understand about that, Miss Council Estate, with your hoity-toity, penniless mother who never owned as much land—"

"Christ!" Joan exploded. "Never owned as much land as would make a fuckin' window box."

She untied her apron. Gemma had bought it for her years ago for Christmas, blue and white stripes. "Debutante en cuisine" was printed across the breast. Gemma and Joan had laughed over it, excluding Dominic from the joke. Now she dropped the apron to the ground and stepped over it towards him. Dominic constantly railed against his wife's laundry habits, her obsessive washing, *A laundry basket in every room, what more would you expect from the washer-woman's daughter?* Now her apron lay on the tiles, a challenge, a gauntlet, a statement.

"I can't listen to it once more. A window box, a window box, a window box. D'you know who else hasn't the land that would make a window box?"

He stared at her, she was out of her mind, semi-detached.

"Paddy Buckley. Paddy Buckley hasn't the land that would make a window box."

"What the fuck are you on about, woman?"

He watched her lift the keys of her old car and step quietly out into the yard. She paused at the door. "Dominic, you've surely heard before that there's many a tune played on an old fiddle?" She was calm as she turned the ignition and pulled gently out of the yard, indicating, as was her habit, though there was no other vehicle for half a mile.

Two hours later, when Gemma asked where her mother was, he still did not realise what had happened. He was furious going to bed in her absence and incensed at his breakfast of toast and cold milk. Later that next day, it was Frank who had the hideous task of explaining to his father what every boy in the College seemed somehow, suddenly, to know. Paddy Buckley . . . his mother and Paddy Buckley . . . he ran out of words before Dominic's howl of rage.

:::

THE DOOR whacked back, bouncing off its hinges as Dilys propelled herself through. "Here we are now, Daminic, didn't I tell you? Here's Gemma in ta see you, regular like clockwork, every Sunday. She's a great wee girl. You must be so proud of her."

"It's no big credit to my daughter to say she's the best of a rotten fuckin' lot. Running around after her husband's father, that oul' crip, Alo O'Donovan, while her own father rots away in here. Siding with her mother, sneaking off for visits on the sly, while I was paying her way through Queen's University. Did I say, 'Yer tramp of a mother's gone off whoring, come home and keep house'? I did not. Why wouldn't she come to visit me once a week? It's the least a man could expect."

Dilys turned to Gemma with a shrug.

"Lovely weather we're having. It puts yer father in such good form. Not that he's ever any other way, God bless him. Never a moment's bother. It would break your heart to see him, straining and stretching, his wee lips twistin', trying his best to say 'Thanks Dilys,' and never a sound comin' out. God bless him, a real oul' gentleman."

She turned to the bed and roared. "Alright now, Daminic?" She glanced back at Gemma and resumed a normal tone. "A wee cup a tea?"

Gemma nodded and smiled.

Origins

::::::

THE HOSPITAL hallways groaned and shrieked by day and night. The delivery rooms heaved with wartime brides praying for good news to send to their husbands serving in the farthest reaches of Europe and Africa. And there were the *others*. The girls like Marion. The nurses were curt and brusque.

Marion gripped the cold, metal sides of the hospital bed and moaned. "I can't do it. Make it stop."

Nurse Josie McConnell tutted and looked away. *Pain? You don't know nathin' about pain. It's barely started.* Josie knew about suffering. She'd been part of the team of nurses which had laid out six members of the Murray family—killed together when 59 Messines Park collapsed—along with seven of their neighbours: veterans of Flanders' trenches, suckling babies, old women. *Jesus, God of almighty, what's after happenin'?* she'd cried as she'd made her way, gasping and choking, through the Derry streets, flailing at the night sky, suddenly thick as soup with dancing sand particles whoomped out from the sandpit at Collon Terrace by one of Hitler's missiles.

While the victims lay groaning in their hospital beds, a sudden and secret influx of American army and naval personnel descended upon the westernmost port in Allied Europe. Barely noticed, they set up covert camps for thousands of men whose arrival was delayed until Pearl Harbor gave Roosevelt the opportunity he needed. Before the fires had finished burning on the naval destroyers in Hawaii, America thrust her soldiers into hundreds of Nissan huts outside Derry. *That's when the real trouble began*, as far as Josie McConnell was concerned.

Marion's mother, Estelle—Mrs Matthew Smythe—sat beside Marion's bed. Sister and the midwives strode impatiently from woman to woman, starched aprons and white sleeve protectors already messed and bloody. Estelle's gaunt face was taut and pale. She took every opportunity to purse her lips, click her tongue, look away.

Estelle had never been in a public hospital before. *In our family*, babies were born in private hospitals, or in the quiet calm of one's own bed. Confinement was discreetly surrounded by flowers and fresh linen with one's son–in–law at his club, or anxiously waiting in the drawing room. Son–in–law. Ah, yes. That was the problem.

Pain racked Marion's body and she gasped, and held her breath, as she had been instructed. She gnawed the inside of her cheek, she could taste the metallic tang of blood in her mouth. From behind the flimsy curtain came the roar of another labouring woman. "Let me at him, I'll rip his pecker off. He'll not get me this way again, the useless bastard. It's the bromide for him, I'll take the lead outta his pencil."

Estelle sniffed. "Lovely company you're keeping, my dear."

The pain was easing off now, and Marion relaxed for a moment. "Is it over? How much longer?" Desperately, she longed for this ordeal to end. Her mother had no advice to offer. "Better off not knowing. What possible good will it do? What cannot be cured must be endured."

Marion had only the vaguest understanding of childbirth. She knew that women died, but much less frequently than in the past. She knew that babies died too, sometimes. Her pious, respectable parents, weekly congregants in the front pews of St Anne's, had never actually uttered this hope aloud, but it had been the bellowing, tusk-tossing elephant in every room for the past seven months.

Please, God, please don't let the baby die. And please, God, let the bloody thing come out quickly. She finished her silent prayer, *And please God, don't let Daddy change his mind about taking care of it.*

Her Daddy's money seemed to be disappearing fast, the war-time bonds and investments returning ever smaller dividends. This year, the double-fronted, bay-windowed house on Belfast's Malone Road had not received its annual coat of paint for the first time in Marion's memory, and Laverty, the gardener, came less and less frequently.

"Daddy, where's Laverty? When's the last time he was here? The garden is a mess."

"We must all make sacrifices," her father said.

"But how will Laverty buy his lotions and embrocations, if his regular employers desert him? He'll be crippled."

Some of Marion's happiest childhood memories involved mud, and narcissus bulbs, and the pervasive smell of oil of wintergreen as the gnarled old man guided her hand over the planting hole. Estelle spoke up to save her husband's blushes: "Nonsense, Marion, Laverty has a bit of housemaid's knee. What? Laverty has *rheumatics*? Nonsense. We can't afford a gardener, and that's it."

Now that money had been mentioned, Marion seized her chance. "I was thinking of applying for a secretarial job, in the Royal Navy base in Londonderry. I need to do my part. If I were a man, I'd join up. Churchill says all of us must help the war effort," she had told them. "I'm dying to get out of here and have a little fun." But the last part had been silent.

Thank God for the job. Thank God she'd been so far from home when she contacted her parents with the devastating news of her pregnancy. Otherwise, Estelle's master plan would never have had a chance. Marion had, at least, the sense to tell Estelle quickly, her fear and shame trumped by the certainty that her mother's indomitable logic would sweep this problem away, as she had swept away the image of Laverty's red, gnarled knuckles, or the chilly sight of the barefoot Catholic children who sometimes struggled to hold open the door of Matthew's car in hopes of a penny. Estelle, as usual, knew exactly what to do.

Estelle sailed into her weekly bridge club. The ladies smiled and chatted as they dealt the packs while she explained her bad news. "Poor Aunt Charlotte in Londonderry is desperately sick, bedridden almost. Typically, her maid has left her, in her hour of need, for a job in the canteen of the RAF base. Lazy trollop, like all her type."

"Oh, not a bit surprising, my dear," said Mrs Johnson. "It's impossible to keep staff at the minute. I'll go three trumps." Her sapphire and diamond ring winked in the wartime gloom of a forty-watt bulb, as she laid down her hand of cards, tightly folded, on the table.

"Spades, I think, ladies? All these young girls, no better than they should be. Swanning around with lipstick, and rouge, making eyes at the soldiers." Mrs Latimer's head of tight curls bobbed in time to her speech; her face, respectably bare, could have done with some rouge, thought Estelle, or even a tiny, discrete dusting of powder. "Shocking, shocking . . . ," agreed the others.

It was necessary for Estelle to move to Londonderry at once and resolve Aunt Charlotte's situation—she might be gone for quite some time.

:::

AND IN LONDONDERRY, ever since, Estelle and Marion had lived in a bitter, hostile silence. Their secret was protected by strict petrol rationing and the horrid inconvenience of travel, in a time when fire engines ran out of fuel and the doctors had reverted to horse and trap.

Estelle and Marion found digs that were damp and cabbage-smelling. The more acceptable boarding houses would not shelter Marion under their respectable roofs, with all the other *decent* young girls. Secrecy was essential, the plan was already in full swing.

Estelle sent weekly, detailed letters to her circle in Belfast. *I have wonderful, astonishing news. Aunt Charlotte's care is so exhausting, so draining, I can barely keep my eyes open. I asked a doctor for a tonic to help me though "the change of life." To my astonishment, he has contradicted me. I am, in fact, expecting a late blessing.*

Mrs Latimer gasped and quickly re-read the tissue-thin, precious pages, crossed and recrossed with Estelle's spidery handwriting. *Dearest Matthew was, understandably, quite shocked at first, but is now delighted and is looking forward to meeting this child of his old age. He is only fifty-five years old after all, my dear Louisa, and in very good health!*

Louisa Latimer sniffed and slipped the letter back into its envelope for further discussion at the bridge club. "Matthew's looking forward to it! Does she think I came down in the last shower of rain?"

Obviously, Estelle's letter concluded, *I won't return to Belfast, for fear of the Blitz—I'll stay here, in the countryside. Aunt Charlotte knows some farmers who occasionally ignore the ration book and slip me some milk and eggs, in consideration of my "delicate condition" and advanced years.*

:...:

A SEARING, ripping wave of agony brought Marion back to the present. "Jesus, Mary, and Joseph!" Estelle tutted and rolled her eyes heavenwards, seeking strength. "Charming, dear," she muttered through tight lips. "Did you learn that from your little Catholic friend?"

Marion fell back onto her sodden pillow from a half crouch. Michael. She could hardly bear to think of him.

All the girls in the base had been warned about the dangers of fraternising with the glamorous American troops. The GIs and the sailors were not half starved like Ulstermen, not shrivelled from years of bread-and-dripping and disturbed sleep. Hundreds of American ships—fighters, destroyers, transports—packed Londonderry's safe harbour. Sometimes the vessels limped into dock, wounded, trailing greasy slicks of oil from their torpedo-scarred hulls. Sometimes they did not arrive at all. The men leaped ashore, once carefree young boys, now rudely awakened; death cheated once already, only days of liberty remaining to them.

Temporary billets sprang up all across Northern Ireland. The men were everywhere to be seen. On Sunday afternoons they thronged the streets of Ulster's towns and cities, desperately seeking diversion in the dour Presbyterian Sabbath atmosphere.

"Be careful, ladies," said fussy little Mr Sexton, head of civilian staff at the Naval base. "These young American men are wild and Godless, drinking and gambling. Half of them wouldn't know a church if the blessed steeple fell on them." The girls tittered and nudged each other.

Bertha Maguire, the grey-haired, big-bosomed chaperone, was more forthright. "Legs together, girls, keep 'em crossed. Them Yankees are out for wan thing only. You don't think the chocolate and the nylons are free, gratis, and for nathin' do you? You'd want to be a quare eegit, not to know what payment's due." And Marion was the quarest eegit ever seen.

:::

MICHAEL (*Call me Mike, doll*) was the most truly alive man that Marion had ever met. All her days of mixed doubles at Malone Tennis Club, her evenings waltzing with the boys of Belfast Academical, had left her unprepared for Mike's coarse, earthy vigour. Every girl in the city was in love with him. He could have picked any girl. He had picked her.

She'd done her best to win the other girls over. She'd shared the precious chocolates and happily sprayed his illegally imported scent on their outstretched wrists. She didn't want to attract hostility from her workmates. She heard them whispering in corners. "See thon Marion Smith, she's the luckiest girl in town." "Who, Lady Muck? Marion *Smythe*? All them posh girls are the same. Hoors, the lot of them!"

Mike was funny, light-hearted, quick to sense her moods and to swing them. Even when they had finally done *it*, he had been kind and reassuring. It had been an accident, of course, the first time. She'd imagined pain. She'd expected guilt and remorse. But he had been gentle and tender. She cried afterwards, so many emotions racing through her, and he had licked each tear away for keepsakes.

"Don't cry, doll, it's always a bit sad, the first time."

"It's not that, not really. I'm crying for my past, really. America's so far away . . . It'll be strange, of course, and I'll miss my family . . . ?" She *would* miss them in a dutiful, filial manner. But she would be with Mike, in the land of opportunity, raising their children under the hot sun of Massachusetts. He agreed with her, murmuring endearments. *It'll be swell, doll, just swell.*

Marion had once seen a pamphlet from the Canadian Ministry of Immigration, "Welcome to Wartime Brides." It was full of nuggets of information about the wonderful new life across the ocean. Boston was very close to Canada, Marion thought. She had memorised some of the helpful tips and new words. *Elevator, bellhop, laundromat.* She had never laundered a garment in her nineteen years; Mrs Oliver came in and *did for them* at home, but the bright, shiny machines in the pamphlet made the laundromat sound like an adventure.

Overnight, Mike's platoon simply disappeared, transferred to a distant location with the flick of a pen. Marion wrote to him daily, swapping egg rations and sugar for envelopes and stamps. She knew that sweethearts all over Europe were torn from each other's arms every day. She was content with his brief, rare letters—he was busy.

Of course she'd been frightened when she wrote to tell him of her pregnancy, but it was a fear spiced with joy and delight. Now, his commanding officer would allot him five days' leave, maybe longer. She wrote to him, *Don't worry or fret about details. I'll make the plans, I'll post the banns. In a few days time, I'll send details—the date and place of our marriage.*

His reply had been instant, and short. *"Dear Marion, I sure am sorry to learn that you have gotten yourself into trouble, and I sure hope that you find a way out. I can't be certain-sure, of course, that you're carrying my child—especially after* that night *at the Odeon. You know, the night you insisted on trying my brandy, before washing it down with port. You've got some stomach for hard liquor on you, lady, like throwing water into a barrel of sawdust!"*

He had underlined the word "insisted" so vigorously that his pen had gone right through the paper. *Who knows what the hell you mightta got up to that night, or with who? As for posting banns and getting married? I sure don't think my wife would allow that!*

The letter dropped from her hands and she sat down with a thump on her bed. Married? His *wife*? Married.

····

MARION ARCHED right off the thin, lumpy mattress and howled. She was obviously dying; this could not be normal, no woman could do this twice and survive. The nurse was out of view, underneath the sheets, *down there*.

The midwife was a young and inexperienced war trainee. She looked round desperate to find Nurse Josie, or even Sister herself, but no help was to hand. Her words cut through the room like a knife. "This baby is black. It's a black baby."

"It can't be . . . I didn't . . . I wouldn't."

"Black." Estelle's veneer of calm, eggshell thin, finally disintegrated. "Black. I don't believe it. I can't bring home a half-caste bastard. The story's thin enough as it is!"

The light was dimming and brightening in Marion's eyes, objects shimmered in a haze. Her teeth chattered and a pulse hammered in her head. She was dying. Black? This couldn't be happening. Mike was the only one. She loved him. She had never been with another man. Unless? Oh my God. She couldn't have? Was this what Mike had meant in his letter? That night he got her so drunk? She remembered the fiery, choking brandy, rushing out to fill every extremity with tingling heat. She did not remember getting home that night, but she had woken in her own bed, fully dressed and feeling like death. Surely Mike had brought her home. He must have. He must have sneaked her in somehow, past the bedroom door of light-sleeping Mrs Mulligan, and laid her down safely on her bed. He would not have allowed her to go home alone? Unless she had not been alone?

"I didn't go with a black man," she whispered. "I don't know . . . I can't remember."

Her mother's distorted, purpled face swam into view.

"You slut," she hissed. The quiet calm of her voice was more terrifying than any amount of raving. "You tramp. You don't *know* how many men you went with? What about your precious Mike? You said you loved him. You said you'd been deceived. This black bastard's not coming home with me, and neither are you. This game is over."

Sister burst through the curtain into the tiny, heaving cubicle. "Silence, at once. Let me see that child." The young midwife sat, mouth open, a perfect rim of white around her shocked, bulging eyes, *Wait 'til I get home th' night, me Ma's never goin' a believe this.*

Diving below the sheets, where the dusky-grey baby lay disregarded, Sister found the loop of umbilical cord encircling the tiny throat. With a practised finger she gently eased it free, slipped the child's shoulders out, and finally administered a resounding slap to the small bottom.

She spoke, loud but firm, over the whooping, indignant roar of the child dangling from her hands. "Now, in five minutes we'll have as pink and pretty a little girl as was ever born on God's green earth. As for you, Madam," she turned to Marion's mother, "I think it's time for you to leave."

Marion stretched out a trembling hand as Estelle turned for the door.

"Mummy," Marion whispered.

Estelle did not glance back, but walked out of the delivery room, and out of her daughter's life.

"Mummy!" It was a howl, a wail one part grief, one part shame, eight parts fear.

Sister placed a slimy, waxy bundle on Marion's chest and she viewed it in silence. Black hair stood up on end, slick with a coating of blood, insufficient to hide a horrid, pulsing, deep-sunk indentation on the crown of the misshapen, pointy head. Her lips trembled and her chin shook as the creature screamed and gulped, choking in a huge lungful of air.

"Take it away," she whispered, "get it away from me."

Sister sighed, sympathy and disgust in equal measure. "When a baby comes in the door, youth flies out the window. It's time to grow up, m'Lady. You're the Mummy now."

The Quare Fella, Part II

: : : : :

FRANK RANG the doorbell, one long, one short, three long.
His car was discreetly parked two streets away. He had followed the text directions carefully. He preferred these expensive
postcodes, the girls had to earn plenty to afford these addresses. It
kept them on the top of their game.

The door swung open and he was not disappointed: a real
Amazon, Polish accent, tawny hair, pale skin, green eyes. Frank
was not a Neanderthal, he was not the kind of ignorant moron
who would log onto the website and make derogatory remarks
about the girls' appearance, their techniques or skill levels, but
still he expected to get what he paid for.

She stood aside to let him pass, beautiful manners a prerequi-
site in the top end of this business. Two bedroom doors adjoined,
their architraves inches apart. Moments too late, he saw her grab
for his hand with a gasp, but by then he was already clicking the
wrong handle, opening the wrong door.

A woman was sitting on the dressing table, fully clothed, filing
her nails with careful concentration. She glanced up. One look
was all he needed. He never forgot a beautiful woman. It was his
wife's new running buddy, Olenka. He was sure, though he had
met her only once.

She slid off the table and stood before him, her taut runner's
body glowing defiantly. It was clear that she knew him too. It

was all over. Fifteen years of marriage, about to be blown apart. Alice would impose a huge penance, nothing would suffice to buy her silence. He had thrown it all away by the casual opening of the wrong door. Alice's suburban life would implode, her husband a cheat and her friend a hooker. It was all over for all of them.

Slowly, very slowly, Olenka opened her mouth and the words, missing the definite and indefinite articles in the Polish way Frank loved, were soft but firm.

"So you know? So you know. Well, is true. I don't know how you find me, but is true. She doesn't love you. She never loved you. Is me she wants. I'm all she wants. Go home, ask her."

Frank gripped the door frame; the world lurched to one side, then flipped back again.

"You? You? You and Alice? In love?"

"Yes, in love." It was a harsh, defiant roar.

"You and Alice? Here? Here in this room?"

"Silly man. Here I pay rent. Here is not love, here is money. I don't take Alice's money, I have good job, here." She paused, head on one side, eyes suddenly suspicious. "How you find me, anyway?"

Frank straightened and released the door frame, a man for whom the riptide had washed over the raft, leaving him standing victorious.

"Never mind how I found you. I'm a lawyer, with important friends. I can find out anything I want. I just had to prove it to myself. Oh no, you can't hide anything from Frank McCann— not in this city."

He smiled and moved towards the hall door. Alice and Olenka. Beautiful, fiery Olenka and immaculate ice-maiden Alice: holding hands, kissing, pyjama parties in lacy underwear. Lesbians. What a joke. Lesbians. Doing whatever lesbians do, it couldn't be much! It couldn't be like *gays*, like *faggots*, doing those disgusting things to each other. Lesbians, cuddling on the couch. On the Couch to 5K. And his own secret safe, the big detective, the man in the know.

"You know? You know about Alice? You know she's bi now?"

"Buy now? Buy now? Alice has always been 'buy now,' it's practically her religion. Listen, not a word, say nothing. Don't ever, *ever* tell Alice I know, or I'll have you arrested and deported. Just keep going the way things are. I'm a good man, and I like to see my wife happy." He closed the door gently, calmly, in her protesting face.

"God," laughed Frank in the cocoon of his car. "Well done, Frank McCann. You're the quare fella."

Bye Now

: : : : :

THE DOORBELL rings, one long, one short, three long. Not my signal. This new man has come for Agata, a referral from our friend Julia, who is leaving town to spend three weeks at home with her children and her parents. I envy her. My children are at my apartment two miles away. I am tired, so very, very tired. Maybe I should send my own children back home, back to Katowice, but my mother is old now, and weary. She has raised her child, she does not want to raise her grandchildren.

I should just go back to my kids, send home the grumpy, teen-aged babysitter, but the memory of the unpaid bills lying on the tea-stained table in the dark flat in Stranmillis makes me stay; *my* client will come in another thirty minutes or so. It is too quiet here today, a waste of my time. It is a chance to file my nails, to glue on the pretty new silver stars I had sent over from home, but I would rather be earning. Or pounding down the promenade in Bangor, with my new friend, sweat pouring from us as we get closer and closer to her big house on the seafront.

A rattle on the door handle. Agata's client opens my door—how can I have forgotten to lock it?—and I jump from the low table with my metal nail file gripped tightly in my hand. If I need to, I know what to do. A firm grip, a short stab, plant the metal blade right through his eye, into his brain. *No, officer, I did not mean to hurt him, it was instinct. It was self-defence, who could think nail file could do such damage?*

The new client has pushed past Agata, no manners at all in this country. I see them every day ignoring bent, old men and pregnant women on the buses and trains. Do these Irish men think I don't see the way they look at me, like butchers about to wield their cleavers, calculating the best return on the transaction?

I have just a few seconds to assess the man as the door swings open. I feel safe in these expensive places; the high fees I charge keep out the riff-raff. The sweat-and-beer-stinking, unshaved Irish men I meet in Centra cannot afford my rates. This man is okay. Short, bald, expensively dressed and *his head up his own ass*, like the Irish girls say, but that's okay. Not violent. I know violence. This man kills by registered letter, by final demand, by twisting the financial screw. He will not hit me, or mark me, so I miss tomorrow and the next day from work. This man is a piece of cake.

They all come here, these little men. They pay generously for what they could get in any bar in town, for the price of a few drinks. I have a regular, Matthew, I know him well. In the Irish way of saying, Matthew is *not the worst*. "Why you come here, Maciek?" I asked him once. "Handsome man like you? Why not find little friend in nightclub?" His round belly wobbled, like a pale pink jelly that has been lain on by a loose-haired black cat, and his chins trembled as he laughed in my arms. "What? An Irish girl? I don't want some fat, half-dressed Irish chick, stinking of cheese-and-onion crisps and falling off her platforms in the middle of the street. Fuck that. I deserve better."

"Yes, Maciek," I stroked his arm. "You deserve woman like me."

This new man has stopped in my doorway. He looks sick. He looks like he will vomit on the white, woollen carpet. The landlord has charged us for cleaning the carpet several times already. That is why I use no oils now, no wax, nothing these oafs can spill or tip over as they writhe around.

I look at him properly, and I know him. I flip through the filing cabinet of fools' faces in my mind, I try to find a context. I have never seen that face from below, or from above, or groaning, or twisting, but I have seen it. It is Frank. Alice's husband. He has found me. Life is either ending or just starting, in a few minutes I will know which.

"So you know? So you know. Well, is true. I don't know how you find me, but is true. She doesn't love you. She never loved you. Is me she wants. I'm all she wants. Go home, ask her."

My heart sings. The worst thing that can happen has happened, and I am full of joy. I did not do this. I did not bring this man here. Alice has told him . . . she is leaving him, she cannot live another day in this lie, this fake marriage with this half-man. She can no longer stay with Frank, who uses diamonds and designer clothes to compensate for no sex and no love.

Joy.

He is speaking. He has found me, he has tracked me down. Alice does not know. Alice *must not* know. He does not care about our love, as long as it is a secret, a little shameful secret. He will arrest me for prostitution and deport me if I tell. The fool. The fool to threaten me. He is a lawyer—well there is no law against a young lady entertaining men at home.

He swaggers off. He thinks he has won. Fuck him, I will not let him win. I will tell Alice myself.

"Alice, Aletta, my love, my Irish swan—"

"Olenka, what the fuck are you doing? I told you never to phone here after three p.m. The house is full of kids. I'm doing the bloody homework."

"But, Alice." My face cracks, my voice is a whisper. "But, Alice, he knows. Frank knows. He was here, and he knows, and he doesn't care. He says we can stay together, as long as it's secret. That's how much he loves you. He doesn't love you, Alice. Now you're free. Free to be yourself, with me, together."

"Fuck sake, Olenka, get off the phone. Have you gone completely mental? Leave Frank? For crying out loud, catch yourself on, woman. Leave Frank and spend the rest of my life scrimping, and saving, and telling the kids *no pony-riding today, no holiday to France*? We can't all make a living on our backs. Get a grip, Olenka. I'll call you tomorrow."

The phone is dead in my hand and I think *he won.* A tear disturbs my mascara and I think *I have lost.* A silver star falls to the floor and I think *I am alone again in this dark, strange country. I should have pushed the nail file into his brain. Or hers. Or mine.*

ICE

::::

THE LAST TIME Mum smiles, it's a pretty ordinary day. She's laughing too, and dancing *the baby-bop*. She's getting on my nerves. I'd pay a quintillion euro and cancel Christmas forever to see her do it again now.

"Siobhan's done a poo in the potty!" The shout echoes round the house, so I pull my earphones tighter. "A poo, a giant poo, in the potty." Mum's face is shiny and excited as she dances round the living room with Siobhan on her hip. The kid's beaming like one of Botticelli's babies. I'm not fooled though. Under that mop of blonde hair and behind those wide eyes, there's a mastermind at work, a genius of manipulation and street smarts. Poor Mum hasn't a chance against Siobhan. Mum's smart enough, kind and all that, but she's no Einstein. Not like the precious *baby*.

The two of them rush off to get a treat to reward Siobhan's brilliant poo, and I huddle up further into my hoodie and pretend not to be hungry.

Siobhan arrived about three years ago; a huge fuss, a rushing, a shouting of *quick, quick, hurry up*. I was dumped off with Mrs Johnson next door, clutching a giant bag of Monster Munch and a bar of chocolate the size of my schoolbag. *Sweet*, I thought, *I love this new baby already.* How wrong I was.

It's totally impossible to understand how Mums behave. One day they're perfectly normal, rational human beings, talking about soccer and *Minecraft* and the *Guinness Book of Records*. Then, overnight, the baby talk starts. Cuddly-wuddly-fuddly-doo sung to the tune of "*Gathering Nuts in May.*" Cuddly-wuddly-fuddly doo? What the hell is that supposed to mean? Who's da precious babba-wabba den? I mean, Siobhan's lying there, she's six weeks old and people're asking her questions and waiting for an answer. Mental. Stark raving crazy.

As for Mrs Johnson? Even crazier. *How's the little miracle then? How's the little angel? Oh, she was long waited for, and hard got. How's yer Mammy?*

How the hell would I know? I couldn't get a sensible word out of her.

All this little miracle stuff is a bit rich too. I mean, I've done *Social, Personal, and Health* at school. I know where babies come from. It's not a miracle. It's not gross either, the way Billy says it is, or funny, like Seamus, sniggering behind his hands and making the girls turn red. It's just the way things are, just like puppies and cats and rabbits. The funny thing is, it's not at all like the birds and the bees, couldn't be more different. Mammals, birds, and insects, what a stupid comparison, grown-ups making life unnecessarily hard for themselves, as usual.

Siobhan flops onto the sofa and I reckon, what have I got to lose? "Give us one of your sweets, there's a good girl. Sharing is caring."

"Mine." She stares at me, glittering flint-grey eyes all scrunched up. "Mine." It's a wail now, she's like a banshee. "Quit your whingeing, I never came near you, keep your oul' sweets." But it's too late, Mum has slammed in from the kitchen, hands steaming and suds dripping on the carpet. "Leave your sister alone, for frig sake, how am I expected to cook and clean if a big fella like you keeps picking on a little baby?"

Honestly, the injustice. My voice is calm, I always try to speak to Mum low and clear, less chance she'll do her nut, that way. "Look. I'm not even near her, never touched her, just told her what a good, big girl she is for going in the potty. Then she freaked out." As sucking-up goes, I think it's inspired. But no, total backfire.

"For crying-out-loud, I've told you a million times. Don't discuss potty in front of her, you'll give her a complex. Leave her alone." Injustice? There's got to be a stronger word than that.

The theme tune to *Peppa Pig* rings out, and I just turn my music up louder—Jim Morrison's predicting The End, through a blizzard of screeching, wailing guitars and the Hammond organ. Mum says I'll go deaf, and fair enough, she's probably right. When I'm learning sign language maybe she'll regret making me endure so much Nick Jr. I've got the message, though; the treats are for the wonder child. I've as much chance of getting a fun-sized bag of Maltesers as the stuffed Peppa lying on the toy-room floor. Maybe less.

Suddenly the doorbell rings. "Dadda," shrieks Siobhan, wriggling off the sofa and leaping at the door handle. "Dadda, I did a poo in the potty. Clever Siobhan. Poo in the potty."

Mum swings open the door and Siobhan launches herself and her filthy paws onto the crisp, sharp-creased trousers of a PSNI sergeant. Sergeant Dolan. We get to know him pretty well, in time. When she realises her mistake, Siobhan screams and jumps away from him. Sergeant Dolan lets a tiny, prim scream out of himself as well, and jumps in the opposite direction. He stares aghast at the parallel brown streaks on his trouser legs like a nun who's accidentally found herself watching a porno, and his hands twitch. How is *he* to know it's only chocolate? He's itching to brush at the marks, get himself spotless again, but it's too late.

"Officer?" Mum says. Mum's from West Belfast, a little terraced house in the shadow of Divis Flats. She's frightened of the NIPS. I know she is, because of the way she tells Dad to *pack it in* when he moans about them. He calls the cops *money-grabbing, doughnut-eating pigs*. He makes *oink oink* noises on the motorway when we slow down to pass a speed-camera van. "They're only doing their job, Matt," Mum says, "they're keeping the roads safe for people like us."

Mum always sticks up for people she hates, or fears. She thinks it makes her a better person than the rest of us. Like making a point of calling Zoe *black* when the other mums at school call her *coloured*, or worse. I don't know if Mum understands the word hypocrisy.

"Officer?" she says again. The smile slides off her face, it slithers away at the corners and tails off into the memory of her muscles. Once it goes away, her body seems to forget how to let it come back.

Sergeant Dolan finally tears his gaze away from the sticky mess on his uniform and removes his cap. He turns it round and round in his hands—a man preparing for his third and last chance to stay in the running for the discus medal.

Mum's face is pale as the china doll, stinking of cigarettes-and-really-old-lady, in Great-Aunt Josie's bedroom. She has big, pink circles on her cheekbones, like when Siobhan gets into the makeup bag and goes crazy. "What's wrong?" It's a whisper, there isn't a hint of Mum in it. It's the cracked voice of an old witch in *StoryTrain* on KidzTV. "It's Matt? Car crash? Is he . . . ?" She glances at us and doesn't finish the sentence. I mean, I'm twelve already and Siobhan's only three, she might as well finish the sentence.

"May I come in, Mrs Jordan?"

"Of course, of course." She's already standing back, moving out of his way, when I cough. That's the first time I ever cough like that. A little, gentle reminder. Things Mums don't think about— they don't watch enough TV, they don't know what I know.

"Mum." Gently, softly. "ID badge, Mum. Name and station."

Mum stares at me. Her face is blank. She's crying invisible tears, the ones that run down the inside of her face, under her skin, 'cause the ducts are worn out from too much crying and the liquid won't come out. But I don't know about invisible tears yet, we're all learning as we go along.

Dolan's face flashes fury, just long enough for me to see the narrow eyes, the wrinkle in the brow, but he recovers quickly. "That's a fine, bright boy you have there. Good man, yourself." He smiles with his lips, no crinkling cheeks, nothing real, just a mouth movement, exposing his long, yellow teeth. He doesn't look at all like a big, bad wolf, more like a horse, but I shiver anyway.

He hands Mum his badge, she holds it in her hand and looks at him for guidance. "Mum." Even gentler, even softer. "Mum, now you ring the station and confirm his identity."

"Jesus, Mark, I can't do that. What will . . ." She squints at the badge at last. "What will Sergeant Dolan think of me?"

"He'll think you have a right smart boy there, Mrs Jordan." The smile is spaghetti-thin and noticeably more fake than before. "I'll be in the car."

There's a dark green Ford Mondeo in our driveway, just right for a detective or an unobtrusive motorway speed-cop. He places his cap reverently in the passenger seat before he slides in behind the wheel. That's when I know he's for real, no con man, no burglar. A real, honest-to-God cop, in a car in our driveway. Bad. Very bad.

::::

DOLAN SITS at the table and waves away offers of tea and biscuits. I plonk Siobhan in front of the telly and sidle back into the kitchen, in case Mum freezes again. Dolan pulls out his notebook and clicks the nib in and out of his pen a few times. It doesn't look like *tactics*; it looks like nerves. Maybe embarrassment.

"Mrs Jordan, could you tell me your husband's name and date of birth, please?"

Mum yelps, a hamster being trodden on, a soft, breathy whimper. "Is he . . . ? Is he dead?" She flushes after the word, you can see she's proud of herself. I'm proud of her too, and I wink her a semaphore of approval that she doesn't even notice. Not an easy word, *dead*. Better than some others that come later, though.

"Not dead, Mrs Jordan, not as far as we are aware at any rate. It appears your husband may be . . . missing."

"Missing, but what do you mean? He left here this morning like always. I haven't reported him missing. Don't you have to wait twenty-four hours first?" She glances at me for confirmation, I don't even have to cough first, she's a quick learner when she puts her mind to it. I nod, *that's right*.

"Ordinarily, one would wait twenty-four hours before pursuing a missing person enquiry. However, in addition to Mr Jordan, who has not presented himself at his office today, it would appear that four million pounds has also gone missing. We wonder if there may be a connection."

Now Mum squawks. "Four million pounds? What are you talking about? Where would we get four million pounds?"

"Not you plural, Mrs Jordan, we are concerned with Mr Jordan only, at this time, and the four million pounds missing from the client account of Jordan and McCann."

Mum scrabbles for her phone. It slips from her grasp, cartwheeling slowly, over and over, before crashing onto the terracotta tiles. The battery lands beside a tomato-stained piece of penne pasta under Siobhan's highchair and the phone-back skitters under the fridge. Sighing, I pull out my own phone and stab Dad's number. It's listed not under Dad, but under ICE: In Case of Emergency. Well, now it appears we have an emergency on our hands.

The phone rings and rings and rings. Mum leans over and silences it with one long, scarlet fingernail, *talons* Dad calls them, the reason why she's always dropping things, the reason her phone is in pieces on the floor.

Cough. Already it's becoming a habit. Cough. "Mum. Passport."

I know where it should be, in the big, red folder from Ikea. The folder has a card with the word "Recipes" taped to the front, as if this tiny subterfuge will keep a burglar from opening it and finding passports, bank books, birth certs, everything that should be carefully hidden in a fireproof safe in the attic. There you go again—not enough life experience, not enough TV, not enough preparation for the worst.

She looks up at Sergeant Dolan and her face crumples. Her chin twists and the skin buckles and dimples into some kind of strawberry-textured stubble.

"It's gone."

That's it really. That's the whole start of the whole mess. No accidents, no sirens, no reporters outside the door yet, just me, Mum, and Dolan, looking at each other over the toast crumbs and the tacky ketchup stains on the table. Clearing the table is my job. Not too proud of my work, I have to admit.

Dolan rises stiffly, with a hand to his back, like a much older man, and puffs as he straightens. He must see me looking, 'cause he frowns and mutters, "Too much driving, son, too long behind a desk." He rummages around in the back of his notebook and finally produces a card, bent and old. "Call me if you think of anything, or if Matt gets in touch." He hasn't really asked any questions. He only came to make sure Mum isn't in on the game and it's obvious she isn't. No one's that good an actor.

Fifteen minutes ago, Mum was dancing in the living room, now she's panting, like Siobhan with a chest infection. Her eyes have sunk in her head and unexpected black rings have opened up underneath, like a top-speed job in an SFX department, only it's real. Dolan doesn't need to stay any longer; he knows what he needed to learn. If Dad's really gone, he sure as hell didn't tell us about it.

Mum realises at last that Dolan's leaving. She's turning his card over and over, like she did with his badge earlier, and he has his hat on his head and his hand on the door before she snaps back to life. Her question is so fast it takes us both by surprise, like a cobra that has hypnotised its prey then lunges in a blur.

"Is anyone else missing?"

Dolan's not as smart as I am; it takes him a moment to see where this is going.

"Anyone else?"

"Yes, anyone else. A secretary at the firm . . . ? A girl perhaps . . . ? An accomplice."

The penny finally drops into Dolan's slot and he comes alive again, but there's no jackpot, no big payout. "Ah. No. Not that we are aware. To the best of our knowledge at this time, Mr Jordan is alone."

I don't know if Mum thinks this is good news or bad. Running away with another woman? Bad, obviously. Running away alone? Without us? Maybe that's even worse. Who knows? Not me, anyway. Her shoulders slump forward and her breath puffs out, shrinking her. I can't help thinking of our unplugged, uninflated Santa Claus lying on the lawn outside, like a giant, red condom, then feeling guilty about the comparison.

Dolan edges out through the front door, waiting to be called back, waiting for the barrage of questions we should ask, but don't. Mum sits and twiddles a loose strand of tinsel that fell from the doorframe when Dolan brushed against it, and I put on the kettle. That's what everyone does in the movies. Nice cup of tea. It never helps in the film, and it's not going to help now, but I do it anyway. Nice cup of tea.

: : : :

AN HOUR'S WORTH of *Peppa Pig* has drawn its tortured length to a close, and now the channel is showing *Max and Ruby*. *Max and Ruby* is the stupidest programme ever made, bar none, and even a three-year-old girl, who stills poos in her pants for preference, is not going to put up with sixty minutes of preaching from a destructive baby rabbit and his smug git of a sister. When Siobhan starts to whine, I activate my secret weapon. Knee up on the kitchen counter, lever myself upright, glance over at Mum for the lecture about damaging the painted cupboard doors. But the lecture doesn't come. Mum's as blank as a powered-off tablet. I pat-pat gently on the dusty tops of the cupboards until my searching fingers find it. Pink plastic and a square inch of latex. My saviour. Siobhan's soother.

Siobhan's more than confused as I pop the do-do into her wailing mouth and drag her upstairs to bed. She's entitled to wonder, I have to admit, considering that Mum posted the soother up the chimney to Santa two weeks ago, to be recycled into new toys for good little girls and boys. Oh, well. If you can't believe in your own Dad, who ruffled your hair this morning on his way out of your life, carrying a passport and a secret, who can you believe in?

She struggles and wriggles and keeps climbing out of bed, but I really don't have time for this, I need to get downstairs to Mum. I fling her back onto the Minnie Mouse duvet and flop down on top of her, pinning her flailing, scratching hands to her sides, and lie there, it could be three minutes, it could be ten, until she gives up and starts sucking rhythmically and breathing calmly. I'd have read her a story, but I just haven't got enough limbs to pin her down and turn pages at the same time.

As I suspected, Mum's cup of tea is cold on the kitchen table in front of her. There's no lipstick on the rim; she hasn't even touched it. In the movies, when someone's in shock like this, they usually get a slap across the face, but I don't think I've got the nerve. The last time I hit Mum, I was small enough to be lifted into the seat of a supermarket trolley and pushed, howling and thrashing, back to the car in disgrace. I don't think hitting Mum is *my* job today, let someone else do it. So I call Auntie Liz.

Auntie Liz isn't my auntie at all, and I hate the way they insist on calling her that. They think it's cute. Liz has one thing going for her: she lives close by. She answers her phone on the third ring, which is good. It took me five minutes with a wooden spoon scraping dirt and dust out from under the fridge until I managed to hook the back of Mum's phone and reassemble it, so thank God Liz is home and picks up. Dolan left here over an hour ago and Mum hasn't moved or spoken since. If anyone's going to get away with slapping her, it'll be Liz.

But Liz doesn't need to hit anyone. She comes into the kitchen, hunkers down beside Mum's chair and it's a tsunami, a landslide of tears and snot and hugging and huge, whooping gasps until Mum stands up, at last, and closes the curtains at the front of the house. Liz struggles up to join her—she's been on her knees for a quarter of an hour—and peeps out through a chink in the fabric. There are no reporters, no vans, no cameras. Not yet.

Liz says to me, "Make us a nice cup of tea, Mark, there's a good boy." *Gosh, why didn't I think of that?* But I don't say a word, just nod and smile, and flick the switch.

We mustn't totally give up on Dad yet, there may be some *perfectly simple explanation*, according to Liz. Mum and I just glance witheringly at her, and now I know what a jaundiced look actually is. The whites of Mum's eyes are muddy and brown from rubbing and the skin round her nostrils is cracking from the rough Kleenex. She puts on a high-pitched, posh voice, "My dear, the truth is rarely pure and never simple." Liz grabs her temples with both hands and shouts, "Don't tell me, don't tell me! *The Importance of Being Earnest*." "Close enough, I can't remember," Mum mutters; "it's Wilde anyway." I don't even ask; Mum and Liz go back a long way, back to College and Drama Club and photos of them in head–to–toe black clothes and white, ghostly makeup. They're always doing and saying mad things, in-jokes that drive Dad crazy. Drove him crazy? It can't be easy living with us.

Liz starts phoning people from Mum's contacts list, mutual friends and old College drinking buddies of Dad's, but she has to stop, because the questions they ask her aren't answerable. Is something wrong? Erm . . . Has something happened? Erm . . .

Ding dong.

"Oh God," Mum shrieks, "they're here, that was fast. Liz, tell them we're not here."

Liz marches to the front door and flings it open. It whacks off the shoe closet behind it and ricochets back, almost slamming in the face of the man on the doorstep. He staggers back a pace and gasps, wiping his palms anxiously on a blue-and-white striped apron. Liz's mouth drops open like a judge hamming it up on *X Factor*, and she growls.

"What the fuck do you want?"

"Er, hi Missus. Robbie's butchers? I usually come of a Friday. I'll call back another day, if the Missus isn't in." He's already turning back to the white van parked across the gate.

"Sorry," Liz chokes out. "I'm sorry. I'm, erm, I'm the babysitter. I wasn't expecting you."

I pull on her sleeve. Cough. "Liz, listen. There's no milk in the house and not much food either, we're supposed to be going to Happy Burgers for dinner, 'cause of the Christmas holidays starting. I can't imagine Mum's heading out to Tesco, and *you*"—I fix her with a ferocious stare—"*You're* not going out and leaving me here alone with her right now."

Robbie's man produces burgers, sausages, and milk out of the van, then stands there with the fan whirring and the chilled air pouring through the open door out into the street, staring at us for ages, before driving off. His eyes are fixed on the house in his rear-view mirror until he turns the corner and leaves. "Christ, he's going to have some story to tell when the news breaks," Liz mutters.

That's when we realise we need to get out of the house. The next time the bell rings it's going to be BBC Ulster or the *Telegraph*. Mum's catatonic and Liz is the worst liar I've ever seen, it's time to go.

:::

I'VE HELPED Mum and Dad pack for overnight stays with Granny, and for weekends cramped in cottages clinging to the sides of freezing cliffs and stormy beaches, but I've never seen anything like this before. Siobhan usually accounts for two-thirds of the packing. "Take the musical Peppa," Mum shouts. "And the changing bag, and the books in the shape of a truck. And the truck that sings the alphabet song, and the doll's house, and the playmat."

Dad sighs, "Jesus, woman, we're going away for two days."

"You're right, Matt, we probably need the doll's pram too, for a two-day stay."

It's not like that today. We're leaving and we don't know when we're coming back. Mum's looking at her hands, Siobhan's back in front of the telly, and Liz and I are stuffing pants and socks into plastic bags. The suitcases are in the attic, but Liz won't let me climb up the stepladder. She just keeps saying, "They sell clothes in Primark, we'll get new ones. They sell toothbrushes in Centra." At last I have to take her by the arm, I have to tell her what she would already know if she had watched half her classmates disintegrate as their fathers walked away for good, after the jobs went, and the money ran out, and the wives started asking them to mind the babies and peel the spuds.

Cough. "Liz." Cough. "Liz, Auntie Liz! D'you think we'll have the money to buy new everything? Do you think a man who's running away on his wife and kids a week before Christmas is gonna go without emptying the bank accounts?"

"Christ." There's panic in her eyes, they slam so wide open that a full circle of white surrounds the blue. "But your Mum has loads of money, she's the one with loads of cash. She's the one with the expensive tastes, I'm the one shopping in Lidl."

"I don't know, Liz, maybe she has money of her own somewhere, maybe not. But we're not asking her today. Now calm down and help me pack properly." And suddenly I'm tired. I'm tired of being the adult. I'm twelve years old. My father's just left me. The police have been to the door. Mum's chewing the white bits of skin round the edge of her fingernails, making a tiny, slurping sound like a prey animal trying not to be heard.

Auntie Liz doesn't have any children—maybe she thinks I'm normal. Maybe she thinks all twelve-year-old boys act like this. Maybe she doesn't know that I have a bad-karma mantra charging round my head. While I find fluffy-bunny pyjamas for Siobhan and watch Liz stuff lacy underpants into a Dunnes Stores carrier bag for Mum, there's a punishment tattoo pounding in my temples and beating time in my brain. *He didn't even give me a hug . . . he didn't even give me a hug.* Who'd hug me, bossy, little know-it-all twat that I am?

::::

DAD'S ONLY a small section on the six o'clock news, just a brief paragraph or two. We're expecting dad's partner, Frank McCann, to be on, telling the country all about the terrible betrayal, and how awful it is, and that everything will be sorted out. But he just says "No comment," shoulders past the reporter with the big, fuzzy microphone, runs into the office and slams the door. The reporter turns back to camera and with a pained, priestly expression reminds us that Dad is just the latest in a long line of *rogue solicitors* to have crashed spectacularly out of sight in recent years.

"Look at that vulture," Liz says. "He's just dying to discover Matt on a paradise island somewhere, so he can get an all-expenses-paid holiday to track him down."

"Give it a rest, Liz, he's just doing his job," Mum says, and that's how I know how frightened she is, too frightened even to tell the truth to her best friend in the world.

Mrs Johnson from next door flashes up onto the screen. I want to hug her. *Decent, quiet, respectable people, kept to themselves, sure it's all a big mistake, I'd say.* She puts her head on one side, as cute old ladies tend to do when they want something, and squints up at the reporter as if daring him to contradict her, but he doesn't, and the camera angle widens and pans out to show a shot of our house, with the flashing icicles we forgot to turn off and poor Santa lying in the wet grass near the door. "Well," says Liz, "there's an advert to show an empty house ripe for robbing." The words are still hanging on the air when the picture pulls back to show a uniformed cop standing outside, hands clasped behind his back, face stoical but raw, in December's chill.

Jill Burke starts the weather forecast. "Look at that dress," laughs Liz, "Jesus." But no one smiles, we don't care about Jill, she hasn't run away and ripped the heart out of the family, she can do the forecast naked for all we care. At once it hits me that we've run away too, and I nearly fall off the sofa.

"Mum, did you bring Sergeant Dolan's card? Mum, we need to ring him. I mean, we've just fecked off and disappeared. They're probably searching the city for us. They probably have an APB out on us."

Mum doesn't even ask what an APB is, but she pulls the card out of the back pocket of her jeans and dials. "Can I speak to Sergeant Dolan, please . . . okay, sorry, Detective Sergeant Dolan, he just said Sergeant to me."

My heart sinks. A Detective Sergeant. In full uniform. This is a nightmare. Mum leaves her message and her contact details with the cop on the other end of the line, but we don't have much faith that they'll be passed on. Mum said she could hear drunken shouting in the background and a lot of clanging and banging noises. The news programme had fifteen minutes devoted to mini-riots all over Belfast, Larne, and Limavady, about the flying of the Union Jack. Mum says we're the least of the PSNI's worries tonight, but I think she's kidding herself.

We have pizza for dinner. We don't even put it on plates, just pull it out of the delivery box and hold it, oozing and dripping into paper napkins, like the guys from *The Big Bang Theory*. We'd never do that at home. Maybe the same thought hits Mum, 'cause she puts her face into her greasy hands and starts crying again and soon we're all at it—even Siobhan, who has no idea why we're having a sleepover in Auntie Liz's tiny apartment, and even Liz, who might be wondering how soon she can ask us to leave.

Siobhan has a meltdown at bedtime. Liz has a tiny room, at the back of the flat, with a single bed for Mum to share with Siobhan. At first, the plan is that *I'll* share it with her, top-to-toe, but I squash that theory. "It's not decent, I'm twelve years old, it's totally not happening. I'm sleeping on the sofa." There's not a lot, really, they can say to that, and I know it's essential that I stop Mum and Liz sitting up alone tonight. First of all, they'll have a couple of bottles of wine if I'm not there to keep an eye on them. Liz is completely clueless, she's never seen Mum at seven a.m. on the day after her birthday, mascara blurred into big, black blotches, dry-heaving from too much Prosecco, and a three-year-old child bouncing round at top volume. Liz is in for a rude awakening.

Secondly, God knows what crazy plan they'll come up with between them if I'm not here.

Siobhan takes a lot of persuading to get into the little bed. She's freaking out about Santa not finding her and Mum's too tired to talk her round. Siobhan has only the vaguest grasp on the passage of time, so eventually I get a page and a highlighter and draw five nativity scenes—one for her to mark off every morning until Santa comes—and she seems to understand in the end. "By then we'll be back at our own house, and Santa will find you no problem. Won't he, Mum?" "Uh, what? Yeah, sure. Santa. Yeah. It'll all be sorted out by then." But Mum doesn't look any surer than I feel.

:::::

IT'S NINE O'CLOCK in the morning on the twenty-first of December and the whole household's been awake since six-thirty. Siobhan sleeps badly in strange places. On holidays, Mum and Dad take turns at getting up early with her, a different parent each morning, but there's no chance of that here.

Dad. *Where the hell are you, Dad?* Daddy? I held my phone in my hand all the long, sleepless hours of dark, listening to the secret sobs escaping the box room. I've lost track of how many false alarms I had, the phone buzzing all night long, with texts and emails and even voicemails. None from Dad. *I'm tired, Daddy, and I can't do this on my own. I'm sorry for all the crap I put you through, for all the contradicting and the arguing and the always having to be right. I'm sorry I drove you away.*

My Snapchat and my Facebook page have gone into orbit and my wall's full of messages of support and a few bits of hate mail too. Some of the usual suspects at school are loving this, rotten little fuckers that they are, but overall, I'm surprised by how kind people are being, especially the girls.

I was with Ciara O'Loughlin the day *her* Facebook page went crazy. We were laughing and joking on a bench by the river, six of us messing and flirting and even a little bit of *meeting* (but with no tongues) and suddenly the phone was leaping and bouncing in her pocket. In the two minutes it took to wriggle herself out of Johnny's grip, take the phone out, password and log on, she had eight messages: "So sry, Hun." "Feel awful 4 u." "Txt me." "RIP K." "Hevn has nu Angel." By the time her parents phoned to say her brother'd been killed by a hit-and-run joyrider, she was already on her hands and knees vomiting her lunch onto a grass verge and attracting a flock of hungry starlings.

Since about midnight, the messages on *my* pages have got more concerned, more elaborate, full-on melodrama, and I know that, secretly, there's a feeling, fear and awe mixed, that we might be dead. Would they like that? Would they make me a Facebook tribute page? All those guys who called me *swotty fucker, Google-brain, Mark-no-mates*? I better post something soon, to calm them all down, but what the hell can I say? *Relax, everybody. We're not dead in the boot of Dad's car, and we're not on a desert island. Just chilling out in Newtownabbey.* Though chilling out wouldn't really describe how it feels. Maybe icing-over?

ICE. ICE. I don't know how many times I've dialled Dad's number since Dolan came to see us. There's no answer, and I know there's never gonna be an answer again, but even pressing the button is an act of faith. Each time I tap his name I'm really saying *I believe in you, Dad. Don't let me down.* I can see Mrs Johnson's face, wide and flat on the news last night: *It's all a mistake, I'm sure.* But I'm getting less sure, less sure than I was during the night. People always say the darkest point is just before the dawn, but that's not how I feel. In the feeble, grey, mid-winter light, it seems worse than before.

In the end, I settle on the briefest of lines on my live feed. We're alive and well. We don't know anything about Dad, it'll all be sorted out. Within thirty seconds, the phone's tweeting, and chirping, and vibrating like a boxful of blue tits on that bloody stupid *nest-cam* web-feed we had to watch in Biology last spring, and I just switch it off and drop it in my ass pocket. The only people who need to know where I am are all here with me. Except Dad. And he's not calling me, not now, not never.

Liz burns the toast and I tell her why she should be eating wholegrain instead of bleached white pan. She scrapes the black bits off into the sink and mutters, just loud enough for me to hear, "Is it any wonder Matt fucked off?" I press a cold, white plate against my flaming cheeks, and I know she's right. Between me, Mum, and the precious baby, it's no wonder at all. Poor Dad. I hope he'll be okay.

Liz must see my reddener, and the tears that are just barely contained behind my lashes, because she comes to the table, drops her hand apologetically on my shoulder, and tells me I'm the man of the house now. Honestly! It should be the priest doing that, it should happen at the graveside, with the whole plethora of cousins and classmates and teachers watching and nodding solemnly. It shouldn't be like this. Liz never gets anything quite right. And I reach up, take her hand, and I squeeze it like I'll never let her go.

"That's right, Liz. You and me and Mum. Against the world."

And it's all nearly worth it, the whole shitty mess, just to see the blood drain from her face.

Planning

:::::

CORMAC PUSHED UP his mask and a drop of sweat from his brow dripped, burning, into his eye. He was wrecked. He should pack up and go home. All the other welders were long gone from McCaffrey's fabricators. They paid him by his output, he could finish up tomorrow. He made up his mind. It was home time. Meticulously, he checked and stored his gear.

He thought about Gemma and what she might be doing now. Because she and Alo worked by the demands of their farm, rather than by the clock, Cormac never knew in advance if he would find them in the kitchen or in the barn. Many a time he came home to find the yard a blaze of light, the house dark, and the spuds unpeeled. He was quite a good cook, had been chief chef at home for many years before his marriage, but food always tastes better when cooked by someone else.

Jamesy Lalor, who worked in the sales office, brought his wife home a Chinese takeaway, or a pizza, every Thursday. He called it her day off. Cormac would like to do that for Gemma sometime, or take her out to a restaurant. They could eat pasta and dunk garlic bread into the thick creamy sauce.

Alo didn't eat pasta. "Jesus," he said at a neighbour's table once, when handed tagliatelle carbonara, "what's this? Tapeworms in turkey scour?"

Once, when she was newly wed, Gemma had offered to make Alo an omelette.

"Ah, no thanks, daughter dear," he had replied. "I don't eat that foreign muck."

She had thought he was joking. These days, Alo did eat omelettes in emergency situations (they were referred to as "snazzy scrambled eggs"), but his palate was still firmly rooted in the potato and in the past.

Cormac locked up the welding shed and sank gratefully into the soft leather of his battered old jeep. Sometimes Gemma would ask him to decline the overtime shifts. She said he worked too hard. Her concern was a little hard to swallow, to be honest, while she was working full-time as a farmer. His wife was a qualified physics teacher. She'd been happily entering her third year on the staff of St Joseph's when they met by chance, at a wedding. Within a year of their marriage, he was relying on her help in the yard. She had taken to farming with ease and flair.

"Dairying is a science as well as an art; and I'm a scientist, amn't I?"

Nevertheless, he had been aghast when she announced her plan to take a year off work to attend Greenmount Agricultural College.

"When you married a farmer's daughter, did you never think you might be marrying a farmer too? Farming's changed, love, it's not all brute force and ignorance these days. I never wanted to teach, that's Mum's dream, not mine." They both winced at the mention of Joan. "The only thing teaching does for you is leave you incapable of choosing a name for your own kids, 'cause you can't think of a child's name that doesn't raise your blood pressure."

"Gemma, love, it's madness. Think about the pension and the long school holidays."

She had an answer for all his concerns.

"If I'm working on the farm, I'll be at home *all* the time. It's perfect, two parents at home, working side by side, and their grandfather too. Lucky kids!"

Cormac, the only child of a dedicated dairyman, had farmed through a sense of obligation and love for the old man, rather than by inclination. After Gemma passed her Green Certificate with distinction, the couple had worked together for years, despite his misgivings and his regret for her "wasted" career. He hated meeting his mother-in-law.

"Is this what I got up at the crack of dawn for, and drove to Omagh College every morning of my life for? So that my daughter could kill herself working on your farm?" Joan spat out the words, lips thin, eyes half-closed. "She has a 2.1 from Queen's University. I'd little thought I was watching her walk up the aisle to a life of hardship, with her good job in St Joseph's, and her husband-to-be farming two hundred acres!"

"Oh, just ignore the oul' bitch," Gemma laughed. "'*I'd little thought*' when I was playing Barbie doll weddings that *I'd* walk up the aisle with my Ma sitting beside Paddy Fuckin' Buckley. I thought the Da was going to break away from me and rush over and kill them both. He must have a bruise on his arm yet from the grip I had on him."

Cormac tried to ignore the whispered slights and smart-ass comments that he heard all round the townland once he quit work on the land. "There's Cormac O'Donovan, the only kept man in Tyrone." "Oh, boysadear, didn't he marry with his eyes open? Lucky bastard."

Because of the begrudgers, he had found himself a job and never turned down an opportunity to stay longer at the shed. He was a skilled welder, fast and efficient. He brought nearly as much money home (in a good year) as Gemma had earned teaching. He'd always run the farm below par. His father and his wife were a superb team. Let them off with it.

There was also another reason for his high work rate. He was saving his pennies for The Plan.

The Plan was a relatively recent matter. It had not been discussed at all until two years ago, although the road to its inception had been a long and all-consuming journey.

In the fifth year of Cormac and Gemma's marriage, their vet had made a terrible mistake. He was an older man, heading towards retirement, only half-skilled in the new technologies of ultrasound and blood testing. Elbow deep in the innards of a group of nervous young heifers, he had declared them barren. "I'll bring them back into season altogether for you, Gemma," he had said, then mistakenly injected half a dozen pregnant animals. All six had aborted their calves over the course of the next week.

On the third day of this catastrophe, Cormac found Gemma weeping in the slatted shed. In the lap of her overalls she held the tiny, perfectly formed corpse of a female calf.

"What a waste," she groaned, a haunting, primal sound. Snot ran down her face and into her open mouth as she gaped like a toddler, sucking in huge gulps of air, and shrieking them back out again. "What a terrible waste of a life."

Cormac had slipped the slippery, slimy foetus with difficulty into a fertiliser sack. Then he picked Gemma up, stiff, resisting, and carried her into the cramped kitchen of the mobile home. Silencing her protests, to the backdrop of her hacking, belching sobs, he had phoned Dr Andrews. Their journey had begun.

They had travelled the length and breadth of the country. They started in Belfast, but had gone as far as Cork. They attended a private, exorbitantly expensive clinic in Dublin. As their options narrowed, they tried less and less orthodox remedies. Gemma had eaten no bread for a year on the advice of one barely qualified nutritionist. To Alo's unconcealed derision, she had abstained from dairy produce for two years or more, spending her money on soya milk in cartons. They had timed things, measured things, taken hot baths, cold showers—every old wives' tale under the sun.

For two weeks each month, Cormac had performed as required. For the other two weeks he lay in bed, hand on his wife's shoulder or hip and listened to her false, deep, slow breathing.

Science had let Gemma down. Her doctors could give her no solace. The same diagnosis came back repeatedly from each clinic, "unexplained infertility."

"That's not a diagnosis," she raged. "That's an excuse for their own bloody incompetence. That's like something a priest would say to you. I'm paying these fuckers a fortune; if I wanted to hear about God's will, I'd go to Mass."

A nice, long, medical-sounding diagnosis would have helped. She could have looked it up on Google. She could have railed about the poxy National Health Service. Cormac offered to take her to the US; everyone knew America was the right place for doctors. Gemma refused to go abroad, leaving the farm, without a syndrome or a condition to treat. It was so pitiably vague.

In all their long years of trying, they had never had so much as a false alarm. She had nothing to mourn, no grave, no miscarriage story to share with her friends. After their fourth cycle of IVF, Gemma looked him straight in the eyes and announced The Plan.

:: ::

CORMAC PULLED INTO the yard and noted with satisfaction the light pouring through the uncurtained kitchen window. The yard was clean, tidy, and calm. It was going to be a good evening.

The old place was falling down, but he loved it. He had scarcely ever lived away, just two years at Greenmount as a teenager. He had willingly rushed back home every Friday evening, leaving at the crack of dawn on Monday.

He and his father had lived alone for as long as Cormac could remember. Gemma used to call them a mutual admiration society, but that had implied an exclusivity that no longer pertained. Now they, all three, were bound together. Alo worshipped his daughter-in-law and emphatically supported the couple in their unconventional farming enterprise. "Why the hell not?" roared the old man, when questioned by unwise neighbours. "Why not Gemma? Sure I've taught Gemma everything she knows about husbandry. That girl has forgotten far more than *you* ever knew about animals, you throughother bollocks!" The questioner would slope off, tossing his eyes to heaven, muttering, "Wouldn't happen on my farm."

She had a wealth of lore also, of local history that Cormac had never cared to know, that Alo poured incessantly into her receptive ears. If Alo grudged Cormac's desertion of the land, it was well hidden. "Go on, lad, do what makes you happy. D'you think I reared you to be miserable, stuck here all your life with me? I'm old enough, God knows, I don't believe anymore in seeking out misery beyond what God sees fit to send."

Their love for the old man had one major drawback. He must never suspect The Plan. Cormac wished that Gemma could take things easier on the farm, but he understood when she said it was impossible. "Christ, Cormac, Alo's as sharp as a nail in a bed of straw, and as dangerous. With all the changes coming, the CAP and the quota, with every dairy farmer in the country expanding and preparing for deregulation, Alo expects me to expand too. He's not blind." Her workload increased, while the old man's ability to help her reduced with every month.

Gemma and Cormac were working hard at faking an interest in the predictions of a dairy bonanza. "I'll not exhaust my precious life, nor yours neither, stuck in the coldest arse of Tyrone, mollycoddling an heirless farm," Gemma had declared, the first day she had whispered The Plan. "We'll keep the land only as long as to avoid the inheritance tax."

At the earliest opportunity, they would sell to a younger, keener man, who would swoop in and joyfully take possession of the well-cared-for herd and the pristine farm.

"We'll pay the capital gains tax and we'll clear off out of it."

"Capital gains tax? The Da'll rise up out of the grave and kill us both."

"Wait, Cormac," Gemma smiled at him, and he felt his heart soar, she hadn't smiled like that for years, pure unspoiled exultation. "You haven't heard the best. We're goin' to Italy."

He gaped, then whooped, he thought the top of his head might split right off, with the big, stupid grin on him. "You're a fuckin' genius, Gemma. I'll draw my last cheque from Donal McCaffrey, and we'll both fuck off to Italy."

It didn't take him five minutes to see the sense in The Plan. They had each other; for as long as it lasted, it was enough. What would it be like to be parted forever, they asked each other, and for one of them to live on alone here in this dreary land, widowed, childless?

"It'll be better, far easier, to live old in a hot climate. We'll keep our windows open and let the warm breeze drift through the shutters. At night we'll walk down to the piazza for a coffee and a granita." They would live in a land which respected the elderly and allowed a widower to play dominos in the café with the other old men. "And if you go first," Gemma laughed, "I'll get a long black veil, and sit in the window weeping, until some rich Italian spots me and carries me off."

They would do it. They wouldn't be missed. His father was his sole kin. Gemma had plenty of family. "Quantity, not quality, in the McCann household," she always said.

Gemma almost never met her oldest brother, Rory, even though he lived in Dublin now—which was just as well, as they were incapable of behaving civilly when in the same room. The injustice of the world rubbed raw in Gemma—Rory had at least two children that they were aware of, one in California, one in New Jersey. If he was of any financial benefit to the kids (which they doubted), that was where his involvement ended.

Apart from Rory, there was Dominic (surely he could not keep going much longer) and Joan. Joan had little enough time for Gemma. She had two daughters-in-law who had given her seven grandchildren. Lucy and Alice would relish the thought of weekends and summers lazing in Tuscany, and Ryanair would bring them out foreign for less than the cost of the parking at the airport.

It was a good Plan, and Gemma and Cormac nurtured it and fed it, and it, them.

Gemma had studied Italian at school. It was easier than the French Cormac remembered hating during his days at Sacred Heart. They had outstripped their basic Linguaphone lessons within the first year of learning. Now they used online classes to improve. It was a joyful project. It was healing them. The hours once spent trawling the web for doctors and naturopaths were now spent learning the subtleties of their chosen home. These nights, when Cormac rested his hand lightly on Gemma's hip, his rough fingers catching and snagging in the satiny fabric as he traced the barest suggestion of a question on her pyjamas, she turned to him with a smile and a kiss. Or she poked him hard in the gut with her index finger and said, "You must be bloody joking? I'm wrecked, piss off with yourself." Then she turned round and settled herself into a nest of pillows. He was equally happy with either response. These nights, Gemma only snored when she was actually asleep.

:::

CORMAC PULLED OPEN the stiff old door which led straight into the warm kitchen. He dropped a customary kiss onto his wife's upturned cheek. He pulled up a chair beside his father and listened to the talk of the day: the chores, the gossip, the headlines from the Creamery newsletter. He placed his hand on his father's shoulder momentarily, an easy gesture born of decades of love and admiration.

Gemma was right.

They could say nothing to upset his father's peace of mind. He was already in his ninth decade, but Cormac hoped that the day of the farm sale was many years in their future. Alo was like an oak tree; his roots held them all safe in his warmth and affection. The now middle-aged couple might be grey and stooped before they felt the heat of the southern sun on their pale, Irish faces. So be it.

Cormac paused in his eating and smiled at the two people he loved. Life could be a lot worse. They just had to keep on planning.

The Letter

:::::

IN THE AISLE behind him in the convenience store, a heavily pregnant woman dashed a bottle of cut-price Cabernet Sauvignon off a shelf. The smash rang out like a gunshot, followed by an uproar of embarrassed apology and sympathetic concern. Jim McCann didn't notice the babble behind him. He was clinging to the counter. A film of sweat appeared over his ashen, drop-jawed face. They had come for him. His number was up. Here, waiting for forty Marlboro and a scratch card, he was to breathe his last. He could sense the scent of death now; it was sour, tangy, tantalisingly familiar.

"Death smells like *wine*?" he thought, as the light faded.

He had been waiting for death for weeks now. Each day was haunted by the fruits of his stupid bravado. He should never have stood up to them. He, who had taken the path of least resistance all his life, why had he opted to play the hero now? His breath was coming in gasps and a dull, heavy feeling spread across his chest and arms. Natalia turned back from the cigarette counter just in time to see him buckle and slide to the ground.

"Bii-lly. Come to counter. Quiiiick. Man is dying."

Billy Johnston had been running a country corner shop since before the word *convenience* had been invented. The obsolete petrol pumps still stood outside the front door; the newly franchised grocery shop had simply expanded and absorbed the detritus and hardware of the ancient business. Amongst the tortilla chips and lasagne sauces, one could still find wellingtons, electric-fence wire, and nails weighed out by the quarter pound.

Jim McCann's mother and father had shopped here when Billy was a boy folding yesterday's unsold newspapers into cones for wrapping children's sweets. There was nothing Billy hadn't seen before. Jim was in the recovery position and clutching Billy's hand like a drowning man before Natalia had finished giving directions to the ambulance dispatcher, her sweet, Latvian voice struggling with the guttural vowels of Tyrone's rural townlands.

"Yer goin' to be fine, man, no bother, yer goin' to be fine."

Billy roared into the dwelling-house behind the wall of freezers. "Aggie, get into the car and drive to McCann's and get Lucy down here. You stay at McCann's with the babby."

Agnes Johnston bustled off, all business. This day's news would spread like wildfire at the shop counter: how her man had saved Jim McCann's life, how she had raced off on her errand of mercy. An hour later, she would remember the slowly simmering stock pot, the bottom burned black and stinking in the dwelling-house behind the clicking bead shop-curtain.

In Altnagelvin Hospital, part of the shameful truth was soon revealed.

"A panic attack? Jesus, no. It was a heart attack for sure. I could get no breath into me at all. The weight of me. Falling out of my standing. A panic attack? Not at all, daughter dear, can I see the doctor?"

Lucy smiled a mortified, apologetic smile at the nurse.

"What my husband means, love, is that nothing like this has ever happened to him before . . . His father had a stroke a few years back . . . he's pretty bad. What Jim means is . . . should we run a few more tests?"

"What I mean is that I didn't have a panic attack, sure what would I have to be panicking about? Isn't everything fine? I'd say it was a mild heart attack . . . angina maybe?"

The hope in his voice pushed Lucy over the edge of her pretence of calm.

"You big, bloody eegit. Sitting there telling us you'd rather have a heart attack than a panic attack?"

Her tone changed to one of wheedling persuasion.

"It happens, doesn't it, Andrea love, it happens to the best of us? Stress. Farming's a stressful life, as you well know."

The nurse smiled and nodded.

Stress, she thought behind the veil of her professional face, *you don't know the meaning of the fucking word. Spend a weekend in here in the emergency room. Then your big, fancy farm won't seem so stressful, with the cheque coming in the post from Europe for sitting on your ass. My ma told me all about yiz. "You'd want til see what they've done til the house!" the Ma says . . . "They've near enough built a new house round the outside of the old one. No recession on the McCann place, I can tell ye."*

She left the room with vague promises to send a doctor soon.

"God, that's a lovely girl," said Lucy. "That's Flo O'Neill's oldest girl. You won't come to any harm while she's looking after you."

Jim sank back into his pillows and turned his pallid face away.

"I'm quare and tired, pet. You go on home, let Aggie Johnston away back til the shop. God help us, we'll be hearing about her act of charity 'til kingdom come!"

Eventually, with much protestation, Lucy went home to where Colette and the boys had things well in hand. With difficulty, she prised Aggie back into her car and down the lane, promising to call in the morning with news.

The evening milking went slowly until Barney O'Neill arrived, unasked, uninvited, and took over, directing the teenage boys with discretion around the intricate workings of the pristine milking parlour.

"Well, Lucy," he chuckled over a heaped plate of lasagne, "Billy Johnston will be putting in for his inclusion in the Queen's honours list. He's that proud of himself. I had ta make half a dozen phone calls, he had every farmer this side of Dungannon on their way here for the milking."

Lucy took a long gulp from a can of Diet Coke.

"You're all great, couldn't ask for better neighbours. Thanks to you. And Billy. And such a relief to see your Andrea's smiling face in the hospital. I said to Jim, '*You'll come to no harm while Andrea's here.*'"

"Och, don't mention it, sure me and Flo is happy to help good neighbours."

She pressed an apple tart into his hands, fresh from the morning's baking.

"Will you have a currant cake? You will, go on."

He took it without pretence at reluctance, Lucy's baking was famous.

"Jesus, at this rate of going, it's no wonder Jim had a heart attack—the cholesterol must be through the roof, living with you."

He laughed to take any sting out of the words and promised to be back as early as possible in the morning.

"That's great," sighed Jim on the phone later that night. "Good man Barney, though I know you and the kids'd have managed. Thanks for everything, pet, I'll be home tomorrow, I'm sure of it. A whole lot of fuss about nothin'."

Lucy finished another can of Diet Coke and went to bed. Colette would be online for hours yet, researching her homework. The boys were on the Xbox—precious little homework they ever seemed to do—and the baby was asleep. She stretched out unfamiliarly and spread herself across the full six feet of memory-foam mattress. The faint, comforting smell of cowshed hung about Jim's pillow as she rolled it into a sausage and wedged herself comfortably, replicating, as well as she could, her husband's round belly pressed into the concavity of her back.

She was sleeping alone.

Sleeping alone for the first time since her last confinement in the maternity ward. Sleeping without Jim's reassuring bulk and solid presence in the bed beside her.

Sleeping in the silence of her own sudden, unexpected solitude, like a woman freshly widowed by an abrupt accident.

Bliss.

::::

In Altnagelvin, Jim lay awake and listened to the snores, belches, and wheezes of the five other men in the ward.

"Jesus," he thought, "if you weren't stressed before, this set of fuckin' cyarns with their monitors beeping and their alarms buzzing would make sure you were stressed by morning."

He still didn't really know why it had frightened him so. The gunshot. Was he frightened of dying, or frightened of being dead? They were two very different things surely. Every day he worked around a hundred bony Holstein cows, any one of which could trample him to the ground should she choose to, planting a small, lethal hoof onto his liver, or his spleen, then licking his face gently as the internal haemorrhage slowly seeped away his life's force. He had been kicked, been trodden upon, been squeezed against the unyielding bars of the cattle crush a hundred times. He had felt pain, annoyance, rage. But fear? Never.

Six months ago, he had woken and felt a subtle difference in his yard. He could not account for it. Everything was in its place, every door closed, every window latched. The cows had been docile and calm. The cat wound herself round his legs insisting upon her breakfast. Nonetheless, something was wrong. The sixth sense gnawed at him. It worked away in the back of his skull, that ancient sense that warns, *Watch out, danger is near.*

After dinner he had gone to fill the tractor and cursed. All gone. The diesel tank was empty, a hole drilled in the side of the tank, making scornful mockery of the lock on the hosepipe. Bastards.

This theft of diesel from farmers had reached epidemic proportions. He was the latest in a long line. It was rife. It was almost like a new tax. There was nothing he could do about it. He could go to the cops and say, what?

"Do yer job?" Or maybe he should say something else. "Get off yer holes and rush out and arrest these bastards who spent four decades killing and maiming in the name of Ireland, and who are now stealing my diesel?"

The cops would make a few notes on their pad, and smile politely. The eyebrows would rise up their smug wee Orange faces, and they would nod at him and think dark thoughts.

Where were you, Jim McCann, when these same fuckers were trying to kill us? When we checked our wives' cars each morning for trailing wires, for some subtle alteration in the well-known topography of the chassis? How many times have you examined the chassis of your wife's car with a mirror on a long pole, before strapping your kids into their car seats? Away home with you, Jim McCann!

And they would be right, of course. He had never been agin' the police, but he'd certainly never been *for* them. They could do nothing for him now. The diesel was already across the border in the Republic of Ireland or in bandit country in South Armagh, being washed of its red agricultural dye, to be resold to unknowing or complicit car drivers at a bargain price.

Jim's left eye started to twitch. His diesel. His money. His sweat and work. His yard, his land, his castle, polluted by the sneaking, silent work of thieves. He mimed a savage kick at the border collie which shadowed his every move, then patted her soft, black head.

"Some fuckin' guard dog you turned out to be, you useless cur. I should never have let the kids call you Patty. We should have called you Tyson, or Killer, and treated you like one. We should have got a bloody Alsatian."

Grumbling, he had gone into the house to phone the oil company and then got on with welding a seal onto the damaged tank.

::::

"THOSE FUCKERS," fumed Mickey McGovern, the tanker driver. "They follow us, d'you know that? I'm nearly sure of it. I often times do see a strange car behind me on the road. I'd swear they follow me, and they note down who has a delivery, who to target next. Bastards."

Jim nodded, the kernel of an idea settling in the back of his skull.

Six weeks ago, that kernel had swollen open, burst into fruition, ruined his life, landed him in hospital.

The tank was empty again, drained. The welded repair had been ripped open disdainfully.

"Twice in six months, ya dirty fuckers. Well, hell slap it up yiz boys, youse have a quare shock coming til yiz the next time."

His righteous anger burned, no thought of fear entered his equation.

"Just put a hundred litres into thon tank, Mickey," he instructed. "Then come with me."

McGovern followed him with interest into the machinery shed. A brand new thousand-litre plastic tank glowed dully.

"Thon other's a decoy. A hundred litres, they can have it. Fuckers."

"Jesus, are ye wise, Jim? That's madness. A diesel tank indoors? In the machinery shed no less. If you get a fire in here, a spark from a welding gun, you'll be blown to kingdom come. Take all your good machinery with you?"

A scowl flashed across Jim's face. His plan, his cleverness doubted. Of course, McGovern didn't know the best bit, the punchline.

He completed his revenge in secret and hugged the knowledge to himself with glee, like a child that has found the Christmas sweets in November and carefully unwound the seal of tape from the bulging tins.

Three weeks ago, he had opened a brown window envelope. It didn't bear the mark of the co-op, or the Department of Agriculture, or any other familiar correspondent, but it did not look out of the ordinary, his name and address typed neatly, showing through the cellophane.

YOU **Bastard** don't

TRY that *again* unless

you

WANT

a hole in THE *head*.

He had seen this note a thousand times before, in movies and on TV. He didn't know the name of the man who had sent it. He didn't need to know.

Ten days earlier, the decoy diesel tank had been pillaged again, emptied. Its toxic contents, a mixture of a hundred litres of diesel and ten litres of battery acid, had obviously not gone unnoticed.

How could they have known? They were robbing yards all over the country, North and South. The quantities were huge. How could they have discovered it was *his* strike for dignity, for autonomy and revenge? Were they chemists as well as criminals? How did they know?

Fear fought with shame in his breast. All along, he had been battling an inner demon, a sad, sickening knowledge that the diesel launderers would never have dared set foot onto Dominic's land. His father would not have stooped to clandestine tricks and battery acid. He would have asked questions, asked and re-asked, his face like a vengeful prophet of the Old Testament until someone muttered a name, whispered a hint. Then Dominic would have meted out his revenge, armed with a lump hammer and his all-consuming hatred and wrath.

Yes, Jim was ashamed. For the first time he wished he was more like his father. A many-layered complicated shame.

The letter was burnt, the tank cut up with an angle grinder and disposed of.

Lucy had been nagging.

"What the hell is wrong with you? Jesus, it's like living with a madman. Jumping at shadows. Spilling your tea. Are you sick? Are you gone wrong in the head?"

Smiling weakly, he had begged for peace, for solitude, for sleep. He had started glancing in the rear-view mirror. He had studied the moving reflections and shimmerings in the stainless steel of the bulk milk tank and had turned off the ever-present radio in the milking parlour.

They would come for him and leave him in a ditch. He was a fool. A ridiculous, creeping, emasculated fool. Forty years of Troubles, the McCanns had kept their heads down and their thoughts to themselves. They had turned out, when needed, to help any farming neighbour; Green or Orange. The more they loathed the man, the more assiduously they helped. Forty years of Troubles and not a slap, blow, or unguarded word had ever come their way or been meted out by themselves. Now, he had brought the attention and wrath of a set of murderous criminals to his quiet home, his family, his small life. For the sake of a barely perceptible, unobtrusive visit a couple of times a year, a few thousand pounds—a crime not even personal, practically a business expense.

They would come for him and leave him in a ditch. Failing that, the breaking of a bottle in a busy shop would do for him.

"Just a panic attack," the doctor had confirmed.

A panic attack.

Panic attack.

Panic.

Attack.

The Oul' Bit of *Riverdance*

::::::

"HAND ME over thon grape, Danny . . . do you not know how to muck out a shed without hitching the bloody buck rake to the tractor? You'd have it done in less time with the grape."

"Where is it?"

"Yonder, it's yonder." Alo sighed with mock exasperation and pointed to the near distance.

"There are two, which one do you want?"

"Thon! Thon's a grape, the other's a bloody pitchfork. Jesus, what did they teach you in the Agricultural College?"

Danny returned from the cluttered, dusty forge full of obsolete implements and handed Alo a four-pronged fork.

"They taught us about grassland management and fertiliser yield per hectare. They taught us about CAP and REPS, not about how to freeze our asses off in someone else's yard. It's bloody Baltic out here. How does Gemma put up with it?"

"I'm unaisy about ye, you wee pup. You'd soon be warm if you hefted this grape for ten minutes, like me, but you wouldn't work to warm yerself."

"Och, Alo, don't be like that, sure I love coming out here, having the bit of crack with you. Most yards the Farm Relief go to these days do be totally empty, not even a dog to welcome you, never mind a cup of tea." Danny glanced sideways at Alo, a hint of a hopeful smile at the corners of his eyes and mouth.

"'A cup of tea' is it? Ya lazy wee blirt, Danny O'Reilly, you're cut out of your Da. I mind him well. Many's the day I seen him, leaning up agin' the handle of the grape or the shovel, breast-feeding it. How long is it since?"

"It's five months, Alo. Feels like five minutes or, the odd time, like five years."

"God rest him. You didn't expect to come home so soon?"

Danny kicked the hinge of the shed door meditatively, an action few people would have been permitted on Alo O'Donovan's farm.

"Ach, Alo, it was a bad reason to come back. And it was so grand and hot over there, and it never fuckin' rained, and the farms were enormous. And I was gonna marry the only daughter of a man wi' ten thousand hectares of Outback."

Danny smiled a lopsided, watery smile. When he spoke again he had mastered the wobble in his voice. "Soon as I met one, I was gonna sweep her off her feet with the accent and the oul' bit of *Riverdance*."

"It was a bad reason, alright, son."

Alo leaned over and squeezed the young man's arm.

"Finish up here, Danny, and come on in. I'll wet the tay."

Slim

:::::

I STOPPED DEAD, my foot on the threshold, one hand still resting on the doorknob. Clouds of steam filled Niamh's kitchen. A huge, old-fashioned kettle rattled and spat as it boiled on the giant oil-fired stove. A flush-faced crone huddled beside the kettle on a pad of folded towels—the witch from Hansel and Gretel slowly roasting to death on top of the stove, rather than inside the oven like the picture books show. One brown, wizened claw clutched tightly the mass of blankets in which she was wrapped, and I could just see the sharp tip of a nose.

"Jesus Christ!" Niamh slammed into my back, slopping Red Bull over her tee shirt. "For Christ's sake, Dad, you're a disgrace. How many times do I have to tell you not to do it in the house? So embarrassing." Grabbing me firmly by the wrist, she pulled my horrified gaze away and dragged me down to her bedroom.

"See ya, Colette." Slim Tim Doherty's roars of laughter followed me down the hallway.

"What the hell was that about?"

Niamh scrubbed a baby wipe roughly over her stained top, sighing and tossing her hair. "Oh just ignore him, he's, like, I mean, totally gross. The sauna at the gym is broken. He's, like, four pounds overweight for tomorrow's handicap hurdle. He's on the second favourite. Hollister tee shirts don't pay for themselves, you know."

"But you can't lose weight like that. That'll never work."

"Oh yeah? Know a lot about jockeys, do you? He's been at it for years. He's sweating it off down there, wrapped in cling-film under those blankets. A few laxatives, NBM, no worries."

"NBM?"

"Oh, for God's sake, Colette, 'Nil By Mouth.' Starving. He'll be fine, it's only a few pounds. By the way, stay out of the downstairs bathroom. Rank." We fell about the room laughing, making toilet jokes and farting noises that were *way* too young for us.

That was nearly two years ago. A faulty switch, a blown fuse, shuts down the sauna in a gym I've never entered, and my whole world opens up.

::::

I WALKED PAST Sean Gallagher earlier today. He was leaning against the wall outside the physics lab, looking absolutely fucking gorgeous. Ok, he's a bit of a swotty genius, but he's deadly popular. His swotty-science-nerd mates were with him, and Kieran Gormley, who, frankly, is a dick. Kieran looked me up and down, he always does, now I look so good.

"Well, stick-insect, how's things?" he asked, "Can yer parents not afford to feed ya? Scarcity of food on the farm? Problem with the cheque from Europe? I can give you a big lump of pork, if you gimme a minute to shut my eyes and think about someone else." He grabbed his crotch, rubbing it theatrically. I sailed past, swishing my ponytail. "Kieran, you're a manky prick," I called over my shoulder, trying to hide my delight. "And I wouldn't let you touch me with someone else's."

Sean Gallagher was staring after me as I walked away; his face was, like, a bit strange, and he wasn't laughing with the others. I know he fancies me. I swayed a little bit from the hips. I know it's working. Everyone's noticed how slim I'm getting. I look *totes amazeballs*. You could swing a coat hanger from my cheekbones.

::::

I STARTED OFF slowly. I didn't really believe you could lose four pounds in a day. At first I was just, like, kidding around.

Locking the door, I slid down onto my bedroom floor. Leaning my back against the chimney-breast, conducting gentle heat from the fire below, I snuggled my duvet round me. I propped my books on my knees and went to work. Maths homework—because maths teachers don't care about handwriting. After an hour, my knees were cramped, my ass was asleep, and I was pleasantly warm. Like, no way would *this* lose me any weight.

Next day, I popped into Johnston's shop for some cling-film. I mummified myself in the stuff. I pulled on an old thermal vest from years ago. It was way too small—so much the better. A few fleeces, and the duvet. This was bound to work. It was hot, it was miserable, it smelled terrible, and I didn't lose a single ounce. I could hardly hop up onto the hotplate of the Aga in front of my parents, and anyway, we don't have one.

Back then, I desperately wanted to lose six pounds, like big deal, now I've lost *twenty*. I'd always known I was fat, but after the incident with that pig, Liam Donnellan, I had, like, a real incentive. Pig. It was gross when I went to meet him. I didn't know boys could be such bad kissers. He wasn't like anyone else I'd ever met. His tongue suffocated me, poking around my back teeth. There was, like, so much slobber. My mouth was full of his spit. It was like the time I had to get my teeth cleaned and the dentist's sucky-thing wasn't working properly. The sucker couldn't keep up, the water was, like, puddling in the back of my throat, making me gag, and I didn't want to swallow it—full of germs—and I couldn't get the probing, digging polisher out of my mouth fast enough. That's how Liam Donnellan made me feel; that can't be right.

I pulled his hand off the front of my jeans for about the tenth time, and I was, like, *stop bloody poking at me, for Christ's sake, like, you're doing it all wrong. I had more fun when I fell off my bike straight onto the crossbar.* He stormed off, and I was so glad to see him go.

Next day, all over school and WhatsApp, Donnellan was telling the world how we had met last night, but it hadn't worked out, 'cause I was so fat. Saying he didn't bother trying to open my bra 'cause the strap was hidden by folds of flab. Saying he liked baby elephants, but only in the zoo. Niamh told me to ignore him, *rise above it*, she said. But he was, like, only saying out loud what I had been saying for months in my own mind. Fat. Fat pig. Baby elephant. Marshmallow girl.

::::

IT'S EASIER than you think for a fourteen-year-old girl to get her hands on laxatives. I started with silly stuff; Andrews Liver Salts, Senokot from the chemist. No bloody good. It was curiosity that made me open Slim's bathroom cabinet—I just wanted to write down the names of a few things. The sachet was, like, in my pocket before I told my brain to think, or my hands to move. It was God, or fate, or karma, whatever. "Klean-Prep" was the name of the stuff. I didn't have the instructions, but I googled it. No worries. I drank the whole lemony litre, retching, on Saturday morning. By Sunday evening, I'd lost three pounds.

You'd be amazed at what people keep in their bathroom cabinets. It's not just laxatives, you know. Nit combs. Viagra. Pregnancy tests. I mean like seriously, my friends' parents having sex—in their forties—if they're not careful, they'll end up with a surprise-baby-Kevin like us. Condoms—I stole a few of those too over the months—I'm going to need them now all the weight's come off.

After six months, googling a new laxative, I found the site I didn't know I'd been looking for all my life. It's A-maz-ing. It's made my life so much easier. I hated snooping round in the bathroom cabinets full of K-Y fanny-lubricant and Veet hair-remover—better not mix up those two in the dark. I was always afraid, stealing. Now I just order online. Epic.

All us girls constantly update the site with tips and hints, and new inspirational photos and stories. I don't know what I'd do without their support. Niamh doesn't understand, she's acting like a total bitch. She just won't admit how much, like, happier and, like, more confident I am now. One day she told me my breath stinks. That's when I knew she was lying—she's probably jealous, all the girls on the site say so. My breath doesn't stink, I brush like three or four times a day, *every* time. Vomiting's so much easier than laxatives, so much more controllable.

Niamh eats like a pig, she must be a size twelve at least, I mean, *hello?* In her swimming suit during P.E. her body is curvy and round, she looks like a violin or something. Double bass more like. Heifer. I look like a model; all hip bones and jutting concavities. I love watching Niamh eat her lunch, she really packs it in. She's got, like, no clue how much more enjoyable it is to watch than to eat. To know that she's stuffing a hundred and fifty calories into her thighs and ass with just one packet of Tayto cheese-and-onion. Sometimes, I give her little bits of *my* lunch, just for fun. She thinks she's depriving me, it's funny, she's so clueless it's A-maz-ing.

Are you sure? And the drool is almost hanging from her lips. *Do you not want it? You're so lucky, your mum's such a great baker. She makes great cupcakes.* As if I would put that crap in my mouth.

Granny Joan is constantly, like, nagging me to eat, to eat, as if feeding us is going to make everything all right. As if it's, like, going to make up for her running away with a *fancy man*, walking out on my dad when he was younger than I am. Is it any wonder he's a mess? Silent or roaring, working or snoring, that's Dad.

And Mum is like a desperate housewife on the farm, baking, baking, baking. But never eating. Standing in the big new kitchen after ripping out the old cupboards that were, like, ancient when Granny Joan was young. As soon as Grandad Dominic had his stroke and went to the nursing home, Mum moved into the farmhouse and ripped out everything, bathrooms, wardrobes, bedrooms. Now the kitchen's full of stainless steel like a hospital; Miele everything. Just swigging Diet Coke and baking, baking.

She added a spare room, with an en-suite bathroom, but then she, like, moved back into *their* bedroom, God knows why. I want the spare room now. The en-suite would suit me fine. I wouldn't have to be so careful, cleaning up after every single puke. I can't have it, though, it's for all our invisible *guests*. Who'd come to visit us, with all that, like, shouting and roaring going on?

If I was Mum, I would never have left the spare bedroom. It's, like, totally beyond understanding, how Mum and Dad sleep together, all that snoring and farting. Imagine, they had sex less than two years ago. Gross, gross. I *know* they did, 'cause little Kevin's only one year old. I was so embarrassed, telling my friends she was up the duff, at her age. Mum keeps nagging Dad to go to the Doctor. I hear them fighting about it. Niamh thinks she wants him to get *the snip*, like a racehorse that's no good, then they'd never have to have sex again. I think that must be it. He just, like, roars: *Change the record, woman, change the record.*

:::::

"COLETTE MCCANN!" A voice rips through the silent class-room. It's Mrs O'Mahony, the old bag who teaches Religion. God, she's soooo boring. It's *her* fault that I keep falling asleep. She accuses me all the time of partying, staying up late, not rest-ing. That's crap, I've never slept better. I must be sleeping twelve hours a day now, including all the little power-naps in school.

Mum's a bit concerned about my grades; they *are* falling, but that's normal in Year Thirteen, it's just a phase.

I'll start studying again next year. By next year, Sean Gallagher will be helping me. He'll be my boyfriend. I have just a few more pounds to lose, then he's bound to ask me out. Next year I can "study" at his house, and we'll need all those stolen condoms—if my, like, *periods* ever come back.

Nothing but My Body

::::::

SALLY CALLS from the livery stables. I know it's her, because
no one else has the new pay-as-you-go mobile number. She
says Bojangles passed his vetting, his new owner is coming to
take him away on Thursday. Thing is, she can't release the pony
from the yard until she gets paid what she's owed.

"I'm so sorry, Alice," and the thing is, she does honestly sound
sorry. "I never had to do anything like this before, but there's three
thousand pounds outstanding. That's a lot of money. To me."

The blood-heat rises in my face and even though she can't see
me, I'm ashamed of my blush. "Sally, it's a lot of money to anyone. It's three thousand pounds more than I have right now, that's
for sure."

"Well, what's to be done?"

"You need to speak to the receivers, send your bill to Johnson
and Lovelace on Peter Street. I don't think you'll get anything
back, though, your bill is an unsecured debt."

Sally is silent, she's hurt, and angry, very angry. It's not like
we're friends or anything, but since the ess-aitch-one-tee hit
the fan, she's nearly the only person left in Bangor who doesn't
cross the road when she sees me coming. Except for Sue. Without
them I'd never get a smile or a greeting at all.

Aoise and I have spent hours every day this week in the stables, with our faces pressed into Bojangles's mane, weeping or

159

just breathing, inhaling the dusty, bitter scent of his skin. We didn't ride him, because I was afraid to antagonise Sally, but we groomed every inch of him and rubbed oil into his hooves, into his frogs, with our bare hands, caressing him, imprinting him onto our minds. Aoise might have another pony one day, when she grows up, but I won't. I can't do this again. I never knew pain could feel like this. I didn't know selling a pony could hurt worse than walking out of your home for the last time, or watching your husband fall asunder.

Sally speaks at last. "Mrs McCann, Alice, please, for God's sake, I can't absorb this. I can't take this loss. It's a small amount of money, but it's enough to finish me off."

I know it's true. Sally's lost a lot of trade to the shiny new stable, *Stars of the County Down*, that opened two years ago. To be honest, I only kept Bojangles with Sally because that's where I met Olenka; otherwise I probably would have taken him and fucked off to *Stars* as well.

When Frank came back from seeing Olenka that time, that's when I started to grow up. Before then, I'd always felt a little bit like a child wearing her Mum's high heels. For the first time ever, I knew something that he didn't know I knew. For weeks I waited for the outburst. What kind of man knows his wife has had an affair and says nothing? I mean, I knew about Frank's women, obviously, but that's different. That's what you expect, that's what wealthy middle-aged men do, you don't have to take it seriously. The hardest part is keeping a straight face when they suddenly start explaining to you that they have showered at the golf club— I mean golf is just a walk in the sunshine with friends, it's not alligator wrestling, he never needed a shower before.

"Alice," Sally's voice wobbles, and she pauses for a moment to catch her breath, "Alice. I've heard you crying in Bojangles's stall. But, for *me*, I'm going to lose them all. Can't you see that this three thousand is going to push me over the edge? Can't you sell something?"

"Sally, I've nothing to sell. Everything belongs to the receiver. We packed a few suitcases, and we watched them tape up the doors and windows of the house. Every single item written down in an inventory. They asked me to help them estimate what my bags and shoes might fetch on the designer resale market. But I told them to fuck off."

I've had this conversation before, with so many people. Friends and enemies. No one believes I have nothing to sell. *Nothing but my body*, I always laugh at the end of the conversation, *and I don't know who would pay for it at the minute, hairy ankles, dark roots, and grey at the temples*. I know, but obviously don't add, how much effort Olenka goes to, to keep her job indoors, off the streets.

God, I miss Olenka. Not the occasional chats, not the thrill of running in full view, dripping wet and throbbing, through the streets of Bangor with my first lover, so little lycra we might as well be naked. Not even the sex. I miss the *idea* of Olenka. I miss the idea that I could bury my head in someone's flesh and howl, and wipe my eyes in their hair, and scream. When Bojangles is gone, I'll have no shoulder to cry into at all.

"I've nothing to sell but my body, Sally." And I can't even manage the little laugh that I usually try to tack onto the end of the sentence.

Abruptly, Frank hauls himself out of the corner of the sofa and hurls himself out of the room. It's not that I've forgotten he was there, it's just that I'm past caring. He's roaring at the kids in the tiny kitchen of the rented flat, clear as day, and I can't even dredge up the energy to go out and hush him. Sally hardly thinks we're the Waltons, anyway. Not anymore.

Most days, I want to kill Frank. We had a deal. It was simple. It was the same deal a lot of women make, I think. I know the rules, and I followed them. Smile. Laugh at the jokes. Don't talk too much. Keep the kids quiet. Pretend to be blind, deaf, and dumb. Ignore the faint traces of perfume.

All he had to do in return was not hit us, go easy on the booze, no gambling, keep his women well out of my sight.

And keep a close watch on the money.

That's all he had to do. Not much. But he didn't. The day Matt Jordan flew to God knows where, via Amsterdam, with the contents of Jordan and McCann's client account, the deal between me and Frank was over.

He had it all set up: retire at fifty-five, live off the interest, play golf. Now he's forty-one. When Bojangles is loaded up and driven away tomorrow, I'll have no escape at all. I'll have to look at Frank every hour of every day, for maybe another forty years.

"I've nothing to sell but my body, Sally." The words tumble out, bypassing my brain, I don't even pause for breath. "D'you want it?" She doesn't understand; a shocked intake of breath on the other end of the line. Too slow to follow my galloping mind. "D'you want it, Sally? You've seen me ride. You've seen me teach Aoise. I'm a better rider than you'll ever be. You could charge forty-five pounds for a lesson with me. I trained with Iris Kellet. That's something those bastards at Stars don't have. And I know *everybody*."

Sally takes her time, and when she finally speaks it's not pleasant. "Yeah, Alice, but the problem is, everybody knows you too. You're social suicide."

"Oh, just you wait, Sally. Just you wait 'til Bojangles starts crashing down every jump that spoilt little bitch sets him at. I've seen her ride, even a superstar like Bo won't carry that sack of cement." And now I have her attention. "Just wait 'til my students win their first rosettes, on their ordinary little ponies."

And the kids will come too. She'll get four pairs of hands, Ultan and Iarfhlaith are going to discover that, actually, they always loved pushing giant wheelbarrows of horseshit round the place. Aoise already grooms, plucks, and plaits like a girl twice her age.

"It's the only way you'll get back a penny of that three grand you're owed. I'll keep my dole payment to survive on, *unpaid intern*, that's what you'll call me." I can hear the cogs moving in her mind, and I press on. "One day, Sally, a lot sooner than you think, you're going to pay me. One day next year, I'm going to walk into that dole office and say, *I have a job, stick your money up your ass*."

"Don't start tomorrow," she finally says, "come on Friday. I'll have Bo's stable cleaned, I'll do it myself. You don't need to do that."

I walk into the kitchen where a sullen, miserable silence has fallen. Frank is buttering a slice of toast on the countertop, leaving a trail of crumbs and margarine smears everywhere. Nine months ago, he had never tasted margarine. Nine months ago, in the house where we'd lived for seven years, he didn't know where the bread was kept. So I suppose the crumbs and margarine mess represent some kind of progress.

I walk over to the table where the kids are huddled in silence doing their homework. Iarfhlaith is the fastest; we've had to pull him out of Sullivan Upper, and now he goes to Bangor Comprehensive, and his homework seems to take less time than Aoise's who is still in Primary school. I ruffle his hair and put on my shiniest, brightest voice. "Guess what, kids? Mummy's got a job."

Frank throws the butter knife into the sink with a hideous clatter and whips round. "A job? For Sally? Shovelling shit? Are you fucking crazy? How much are you getting?"

"I'm getting nothing, Frank. We owe her three grand." He throws his hands up and sighs. "Working for nothing. Jesus Christ."

"That's right, Frank. Working for nothing. Just like you did for the last twenty years. Don't worry about it. That's what you always said to me, *Don't worry about it*, you said, *Matt's the money-man, I'm the glamour.* Well, I'm going to be Sally's glamour."

He clenches his fists. Really tight, as if he might hit me for the first time. Suddenly, he relaxes his hands and bites a huge lump out of his toast. Through a mouthful of wholegrain, he says, "Best of luck with your new job, if you're fuckin' fool enough to go through with it."

I go into the "master" bedroom, which is smaller than the smallest bathroom in the house I still think of as home, and I hug myself tightly and try to get my shallow, rapid breaths back under control. I have a job. I've never been so frightened or excited in my life. I am not Frank McCann's wife. I have a job. I am Alice McCann. I have nothing to sell but my body.

Bleeding

::: :: :::

BLOOD SPLASHED onto the crumpled, white bedcover, an obscene bouquet tossed onto snow. Cathy touched her face in wonder, before rushing to the bathroom. She turned the key in the only door which locked; a fiction of security. Already the blood was slowing down. She could count each separate drop. So her nose was not broken then, a few burst capillaries, nothing worse. She might not even have a bruise tomorrow, a stroke of good luck.

Gripping both sides of the basin, she forced her head up and looked appraisingly at the woman in the mirror. The face was recognisable, clearly the face that smiled out from her passport, unless she stared hard into her own eyes, which she tried to avoid these days.

"What the fuck am I doing?" The high-pitched whine ripped unbidden from her throat. "Where am I, will I ever come back?"

He was roaring from the bedroom, demanding her return, but she was under no illusions. She would not open this door yet. She was safe. He was safe. He could not crash his shoulder through the flimsy plywood of the door, like a soap opera villain. Nor could he sit outside, flattering and cajoling, until she relented and turned the key. He could not come after her. He could not intrude upon her wounded solitude. She was safe. He was safe.

The noise levels were abating outside her sanctuary; he had roared and raged himself quiet. He always did, given enough time and space. The thought of opening the door filled her with horror. Could she stay here forever? She had water, she could hide for days. Who would notice? Well, *he* would, obviously, but did she care? Could she bring herself to care? Perhaps a day or two without her would do him some good.

She could go to the police. She could push him, in his chair, through the doors of the police station and show them her bloodied face and clothing. He would sit, head lolling in his wheeled chair, so weak, so vulnerable; they would think she was crazy.

The crusted blood washed away easily enough from her lips and chin. Her top was ruined but it was only a cheap rag, really, almost disposable. She thought, momentarily, of her wardrobe full of filmy, flattering clothes. Karen Miller and Coast mainly, and a few treasured pieces with real designer labels for big days— for closing deals, presenting to the partners, or lunching with clients. She had not wasted her good clothes on small fry; only the biggest chequebooks had inspired her to dress powerfully. On normal days, she had aspired simply to look calm, competent: reliability personified. She allowed herself a wry, bitter smile as she scrubbed ineffectually at the blood on her chain-store tee shirt and tracksuit. It was the first she had ever bought, six months ago; now she had a small collection.

::::

THE MEMORY of those first, heady days last year with Rory was like a movie, a big-budget, 3D movie of someone else's life. His touch, his smile, her joy. He taught her, at last, to stagger with desire, and to tremble, fully dressed. She'd been so grateful. She'd been delirious with her discovery.

Perhaps, if she'd been younger . . . Perhaps, if she'd not already endured civilised and urbane relationships, with civilised and urbane men, Rory might have just passed on. She might have relegated him to a racy water-cooler anecdote. To meet a man like him, at her age, at her stage, had been a wholesale, headlong,

Damascene conversion. They had spent their weekends in bed—sore, drenched, and stinking. *This beats comparing focaccias in some terrible farmers' market with John or David*, she thought, wrapping his dark whorls of hair round her fingers, sighing, gasping with exhaustion.

She had stopped trying to educate him, this man who thought Anna Netrebko and Cecilia Bartoli might be runners in the maiden hurdle at Chepstow, but who had grudgingly confessed to a vague familiarity with Luciano Pavarotti, *that fat fucker*, and to being able to hum a few bars of "Nessun dorma."

She had stopped cooking him risotto, had stopped carefully infusing fish stock with perfectly drinkable wine. She had just gone along madly. Rory was the only man she had ever known who would rip a fifty-euro pair of La Perla cami-knickers down the seam with impatience for her. For her! She couldn't bring herself to regret it all, not just yet.

Rory had damaged her, though. It was undeniable—she was not stupid, nor a hypocrite. She could not stand in a locked bathroom, wiping blood off polycotton, and pretend to be a confident, successful, thirty-nine-year-old career girl. Everything had changed since her mistake, the stupid, avoidable accident that had wrecked everything between them. Overnight, their lives had changed, the relationship destroyed utterly. Now she was worthless, used up, worn out. As if that monster in the other room was going to congratulate her on a deal closed, on another grinding step towards the glass ceiling.

Scarcely breathing, she slipped out of the tiny en-suite bathroom, past the bed where *he* lay sleeping. Her face puckered at the sour, bitter smell of the room. She paused for just a moment. Gazing down at the bloodied bedding, she felt a stab of disbelief. She touched her swollen, painful face. It had really happened. She cringed, recalling the way he had looked at her, his candid blue eyes, so calm, so unhurried, before smashing his head into her face. There could be no apology, no acknowledgement at all, and she was a fool to think of it. If some other abject madwoman would take on her role, service his endless needs, he would never think of her again, nor register her absence.

A glistening string of saliva stretched from his slack mouth to the white sheet beneath him. It pulsed with his breathing. It elongated with each tiny twitch of his lips and yet did not sever. It might last forever, bound to this casual, cruel monster, as surely as she was. She imagined herself, struggling here forgotten in slimy, sticky bondage, while all around her the world turned regardless.

Her thoughts deepened and darkened, as so many times before. The clarity, the vividness always frightened her. It seemed less an imagining than a memory, or a premonition. There was no one she could talk to, no friendly soul would extricate her from this mess of her own making. To whom could she utter the words? Her shaking hands picked up a pillow, so light, so insubstantial. Could it really be done? She imagined placing the square of fabric and feathers over the rounded, pretty face she had come to loathe, breathing fast, pushing down with all her weight, until he stiffened, then sagged, beneath her.

In the living room, she sat in her favourite chair, clinging to its arms as though to a life raft. Her chest seethed up and down, a small boat on a terrible storm, the single occupant clinging to her sanity in the maelstrom. She must stop this image in her head. She must get help. *There must be other women who feel this way, I cannot be alone*—but she knew she was lying to herself. He was a monster, and she was growing to hate him more with each passing day.

Looking round, she was crushed by the filth of her home. It was beautifully proportioned and she had furnished it lovingly with taste and flair. Her apartment was unusually large in a ruinously expensive Dublin suburb. *My flat*, as she always described it, with a self-deprecating smile, knowing her guests would gasp in shocked delight as she threw open the door for them.

It was a small pleasure, but important to her. She had never been wealthy, nor poor. Her parents would have described their lives as *comfortable*, had they ever known anyone crass enough to ask. She had slaved and struggled to shed that label of *comfort*.

Her parents, in Fermanagh, had been hungry, chilled-to-the-bone children of the early postwar period: ration cards, dried eggs, and no toothpaste. When they landed the holy grail of Civil

Service posts, they'd filled their small home to bursting: *Look at us . . . we drink wine at Christmas . . . we serve the parish priest scones on Royal Albert dishes . . . we replace our wedding presents if they break.* How abruptly, how exultantly, she had shed off their accumulated ornaments, their seaside knickknacks. Every item on display in her apartment had been carefully, and painstakingly, arranged to an expensive and artful air of casual chic. Without hesitation, she had sent her late mother's collection of heavily cut crystal to the salesroom, and her Aynsley porcelain to Oxfam.

So she was truly shaken as she looked properly at her surroundings for the first time in days. The treasures she had carefully and wisely accumulated were still here, but soiled, spoiled. The unmistakable odour of vomit hung in the air. The whole place stank of vomit, piss, and shit, she noted—shocked at the vulgarity of her inner monologue. A few months ago she would have said (and even thought) *poo* and *wee*. Everything was coarsening; she fastest of all. She noticed a discarded bottle, flung aside in a rage, or simply dropped out of his hands. From the bottle coursed a filthy trail, snaking down over the upholstery of the sofa and onto a pale, stinking pool on a white rug. The rug was worth a month's mortgage repayment. Not any more, of course.

There is no one I could tell, she thought again. Who would believe it? More importantly, who could view this wreckage and resist the temptation?

We told you, they would say with quiet satisfaction, *We warned you. It was not too late.*

"Well, it's too late now," she muttered. "I made my own bed. I took Rory to my bed. I hung off it, and gasped in it, and screamed in it. Now that it has become a bed of nails, I will still lie in it." *So much for education, and emancipation. Some essential things do not change.*

"That creature sharing my room is a monster, a parasite. I've changed my world for him, and the world couldn't care less."

Her head shot up, triangulating the unmistakable sound of *him* stirring. She leaped to her feet and ran to the galley kitchen. She toyed momentarily with the idea of scalding him. Just a moment's passing fancy. She was not so far gone. She still knew right from wrong, and while she still could, she would behave appropriately, whatever the provocation. Begging the kettle to boil, the task to flow smoothly, she knew that if she was fast, and lucky, she might forestall the next fury.

She could buy some time, placate him, maybe even make him smile. Then she would clean up, and tidy. She would bleach the bloodstains. She would make it better between them. It would work. She would make it work. It was the most natural thing in the world. Other women coped; she would too. Grabbing the warm drink and some paracetamol, in case he needed it, she approached the bedroom door cautiously.

Peering round the door, she thought, *I might not be too late. He looks okay. He's not angry yet, he's not fully awake.*

"I can do this," she swore aloud, "I can keep doing this forever. I love him. Yes, I do. I love him. I think so, anyway. If he would just give me the slightest hint that he loves me too. I *could* love him. I will love him, if it kills me."

If only Rory were here with me. If he had only stayed with me. If he had helped. If he had not left me here, trapped with this monster.

She entered the room, flung open a window, and drank in the icy air before walking to the bloodied cot. "Hush, darling. Mummy is here."

The Accidental Wife

Thanks

With thanks to

David Butler, who taught me what little I know.

Margaret Scott, the first person to know about, and encourage, my secret writing habit.

Liz Nugent, whose kindness and generosity to a virtual stranger appear to know no bounds.

Martina Devlin, who has faith in me.

Anthony J. Quinn, whose kind words and support mean a lot.

The world of Irish writers online and especially on Facebook—a kinder and more welcoming group of people cannot be imagined.

Debra Leigh Scott and Hidden River Arts, Philadelphia, for entrusting their reputation to my first work.

The indefatigable Paul McVeigh, through whose invaluable website of writers' resources I discovered the Eludia Award.

All the editors who allowed me space in their journals.

The members of Liffey Writers Circle who tolerate my erratic attendance.

And finally and most importantly, my tolerant family and friends, who endured the long gestation of *The Accidental Wife and Other Stories*.

An Interview
with the Author

Q: Congratulations on winning The Eludia Award, 2014, with this, your first full-length work of fiction. The Eludia Award is presented annually to a woman who comes to publication slightly later in life. Did you always know that you would be a writer?

Orla: That is an interesting question. I don't think of myself as a writer, and perhaps I never will. I know many writers who have been filling notebooks and drafting stories since they could hold a pencil. That's not me. I always knew that I could make words do what I wanted, but I have never thought of myself as a writer.

Q: To me that sounds a little bit like "imposter syndrome." Your first book is in your hands and others have been written and are awaiting publication, so why don't you think of yourself as a writer?

Orla: If I were allowed to choose only one word to describe myself, it wouldn't take me five seconds to choose it. And (rather horrifyingly, perhaps) it wouldn't be "mother"—hello kids, mummy loves you, really. It wouldn't be "wife" or "writer" or "singer," or "homemaker" or "friend," although I am all of those things to the very best of my ability. The only word I could truly choose is *reader.* I started school at three years of age and I have had a book in my hand ever since. I feel lucky to have been a child when there were only approximately two million books available in the English language and when my scope was somewhat bounded by the confines of the local public library and the school library. It meant that I had no choice but to read the classics, because that's what was available. And it also meant that the library staff knew me and facilitated my reading in every way, and allowed me to take books from the adult section many years before I was technically permitted to do so. In that way, I had guidance but almost limitless access.

Q: Do you feel libraries still have an important role to play, or are they obsolete with the arrival of digital downloads and online bargain bookstores?

Orla: Whether we want free, open spaces where a low-income child can explore the vast hive-mind of the world of literature, and where cold, hungry people can read a magazine or snooze on a comfortable chair out of the rain, is a moral question rather than a literary question. My answer would be "Yes." But, beyond that, I think the most essential function of a library is not to hand out physical books, or give people access to the internet and host knitting clubs, although all these functions are great. The most important thing about libraries is that they contain librarians. And a good, well-motivated librarian is a great gift to a town or district. It is heartbreaking to see library branches closing or curtailing their hours. Librarians and booksellers are essential services, as important to the emotional and spiritual health of a district as public sports facilities are to its physical health.

Q: Well, now that your own book is heading into the public libraries, how does that make you feel?

Orla: It's absolutely terrifying. I am torn between wanting everyone in the world to read it and hoping that no one ever does. The book focuses on one wholly fictional extended family in Northern Ireland, doing their very best to just get along and face each day as it comes. And Northern Ireland is a very small place. If I had set out to write a comfortable book, I would have set it somewhere else. I know every author has to deal with people who feel that their work of fiction is not particularly fictional at all, and the events of the period 1965–2000, approximately, in Northern Ireland contain a lot of shared hurts and a huge amount of painful shared experiences.

Q: Does that mean that you have written the stories of people you know?

Orla: No, to the largest extent possible I have written my own stories through the eyes of my characters. But some events were pretty universal and some fears were absolutely shared among the entire population. Every single person of my age or older knows someone who died, or was injured, or who committed these awful crimes, or ministered to the wounded. It's not possible to write a book about Northern Ireland's Troubles without stirring up memories belonging to other people. At one point in the book, a farmer is robbed by paramilitaries, and literally dozens of farming families could claim that as their own story. My late uncle was one of those farmers, and although I haven't written his story, of which I don't truly know the details, it was impossible to write that story without thinking of my uncle and his suffering and all the things that were never spoken of in public.

Q: So people can relax then? You haven't "put them" in your book?

Orla: There is one story in the book where the narrative device genuinely belongs to another person. The first story in the collection, "Strike," was written a full year after the rest of the book, when I learned that I had won the Eludia Award and that the book would be published. Although the characters and the relationship in the story are entirely fictional, the plot device is a family story belonging to my mother. I wrote the story very deliberately as a tribute to my mother and to the tens of thousands of ordinary, quiet, and incredibly brave mothers who got on every day with the endless tasks of child-raising and homemaking and going out to work, under the most extraordinary circumstances. So, Mum, if you've read this far, thanks for everything.

Q: And what's next? Do your other books deal with the same thorny issues?

Orla: Well, the next book that will see the light of day couldn't be more different. It's called *The Flight of the Wren* and it's based primarily in County Kildare, where I have lived for about fifteen years, at the time of the Irish Famine. I've included a few pages of the first chapter at the end of *The Accidental Wife*, in case anyone makes it this far and wants a little taste of what's to come.

Q: That's a massive departure from this short story collection . . .

Orla: There's a cliché that everybody's first book is a poorly disguised autobiography and, actually, so are all their others, except that the disguise gets better. I really do hope that's not going to be the case with my work, and I feel that might have something to do with the fact that I have actually written my autobiography, or at least a full-length memoir. I hope that between the memoir and this collection, I have got it out of my system.

Q: And when will the memoir be available?

Orla: Never. I wouldn't publish a memoir about Northern Ireland. I don't believe the society is stable enough yet for me to go rocking the boat with my memories, which aren't of national or international significance. If political figures and other public figures feel that they can contribute to the wider discourse by publishing their life stories, I understand that, but my memoir isn't for public consumption. It was extremely interesting to write, though, as I imagined that it would be a very angry and bitter book, and it actually turned out quite light-hearted and full of love and joy, which reflects my very, very lucky existence during the Troubles, when all around was falling apart. I and all my friends and loved ones seemed somehow to have a charmed existence, and we all pulled through, more or less unscathed. If anyone is interested in the memoir, I have published a few snippets here and there, and the links are available on my website, www.orlamcalinden.com.

Q: What are you going to do right now, when the interview ends? More writing?

Orla: I am going to collect the youngest of my four young children from school, and that's the end of writing for today. Maybe for the rest of the week, or longer. There's always time for reading, but not always for writing. The children know that when I have a novel in my hand and a particularly glazed expression in my eyes, all bets are off—it might be cheese on toast for dinner tonight.

For Readers and Book Clubs

Questions to Discuss or Think About

1. Why did you choose to read this book?
2. Do you have any experience of Northern Ireland's Troubles or another conflict? If so, did you recognise any similarities?
3. Would the book encourage you to read other literature on this topic?
4. Do you have strong feelings about the identity of people who live in Northern Ireland? Some identify as British, some as Irish, and some, increasingly, as Northern Irish. Do you think these distinctions still matter in the globalised world?
5. The book features the voices of several children and teenagers. In "Control Zone," eight-year-old Gemma adores her father, Dominic. In "The Reluctant Farmer," sixteen-year-old Rory loathes Dominic. Do you feel their different attitudes to their father are caused by age or gender or another reason? Does this different perception of the parent ring true for you?
6. There are several rather different marriages discussed in the book. Which marriage did you find most interesting? Which did you find most realistic? Do you think these marriages might have played out differently in a less stressful environment?

Contacting the Author

If you would like to contact the author, comment on this book, receive advance notice of new publications, or arrange a reading or a book-club evening with the author (and a couple of bottles of wine), contact her at orlamcalindenauthor@gmail.com.

Keep your eyes open for special offers and news at the author's website: www.orlamcalinden.com.

Further Reading

Here are some of Orla's favourite books, old and new, about Northern Ireland:

The Good Son by Paul McVeigh (a sensitive young boy comes of age in West Belfast)

The House Where It Happened by Martina Devlin (historical novel about the only witch trial in Ulster)

Disappeared by Anthony J. Quinn (Detective Celcius Daly tries to unravel the past in post-Troubles Northern Ireland)

Burning Your Own by Glenn Patterson (coming of age in the loyalist tradition)

Matters of Life and Death by Bernard MacLaverty (short story collection)

December Bride by Sam Hanna Bell (a true classic of Irish writing)

Any work from the pens of Sam McAughtry, Benedict Kiely, and of course Seamus Heaney

And for children:

Across the Barricades by Joan Lingard (YA fiction, love across the sectarian divide)

Mark Time by Sam McBratney (world-famous author of *Guess How Much I Love You*)

The Flight of the Wren

Exclusive Free Sample

The following is an exclusive free sample of *The Flight of the Wren*, coming soon from the same author. Follow www.orlamcalinden. com to keep up to date with *The Flight of the Wren*.

Chapter One

Parish of Clonsast, King's County, October 1848

My parents' grave made an uncomfortable bed. I couldn't keep doing this, lying here night after night under the stars. It was late October and my thin, ragged dress offered so little protection that, one night, I was just going to slip away and join the corpses under the soil if I wasn't careful.

I pulled myself off the damp, cold ground. On the soft mound of earth below me, clear and slight, the imprint of the small weight of my body. Beneath the rough wall which enclosed the small field I knelt and began to search for stones. I rejected stone after stone until at last I found one, a white-grey, smooth slab, as large as my own head, and so heavy that I couldn't lift it, but tugged, pushed, and dragged it from the field margin to the mound of earth. It flopped onto the recently dug earth, and sank a little before bedding down and settling.

The flat, blanched stone was one of the few markers in the soft earth of the paupers' section of the boneyard, and I wished I could carve their names on it. Matthew and Norah Mahon, dead as dreams, blackened and bloated, waiting under the lightly tamped earth for the next penniless corpse to come along to be buried at the expense of the Parish of Clonsast in King's County. And that would be soon enough.

Keep that man out of the house, my father had roared at the first sight of the stranger. *We've nothing to share, let him go on his way*. But my mother had shared the only thing we had, a few smoky flames from a bog-damp, peat-sullen fire in the middle of the hut. The stranger had barely spoken, wheezing and panting away the short autumn day in the silky ashes, before sidling out at dusk to slip round the barricades thrown up by Reverend Henry Joly's men to protect the village from road fever. He paused on the threshold to leave us his blessing. And typhus. My parents were buried within three days of each other. And I was still alive. Alive and hungry.

At the boundary hedge of a field close by the boneyard I gathered some late blackberries. The berries were almost finished for this year; half the fruits I gathered had a fat, glistening maggot hidden within them, and the birds had had their share too. I washed the few good fruits down with a fistful of water from a fast-flowing stream. The girl in the water stared back at me, wasted, wan, tear-tracks running through the dirt plastered to her cheeks. I splashed my face and rubbed some colour back into my skin until I looked healthy enough. My parents were five days, and two days, dead by now, and I was showing no signs of typhus. I wasn't going to die this time, and lying on the ground, weeping, would not feed me. My freezing feet stung and burned as I passed, wraith-light, over the hoar-rimmed ridges of the field, and slipped into the still-sleeping village of Clonbullogue.

"Thomas," I called, half-hidden behind the wall of the baker's house, "Thomas Crampton, it's me, Sally Mahon. Could you spare me a crust, for the love of God?"

Thomas drew a quick, hissing breath through his teeth, quickly made the sign of the cross, and followed it with a sign to ward off the evil eye, even though he knew that Father John would rant and rave from the pulpit if he heard about it. He silently hacked the heel off a loaf and glanced in my direction.

"In the name of God, get away from my door, girl," he hissed. "Who will buy my bread if they see the child of the typhus house standing by the oven?"

He raised his right arm and I shrank back, expecting a slap. Instead, he threw, as hard as he could, and the precious bread sailed past me and landed on the ground five feet away.

"Get away now, girl, get away. Come back tomorrow, but come in the dark of the morning."

"May God be good to you, Tom Crampton," I called back. "Bless you." I brushed the dirt of the road off the precious bread, stuffed it down the front of my dress, and ran.

When the bread was gone, I cleaned myself up a little in the stream. I needed to be decent, in case the people would let me back into the village. I walked with weary legs the half-mile distance to my mother's cabin, on the edge of the bog of Allen, half-expecting the cabin to be gone. The word had come out from Joly's agent that typhus cabins were to be knocked down and burned, over the bodies of the dead, to stop the new scourge of the road fever. For the same reason, a barricade had been thrown up on both sides of the villages to keep the starving, filthy wanderers away, even though some slipped through, like the man who had killed my parents. The men of the burial crew—just angry, anxious eyes flashing above mouths and noses well wrapped in vinegar-soaked scarfs—had not come within the walls of the cabin, but had ordered me to drag out, first my father, then my mother, and heave them up, stiff and brittle as kindling, onto a cart. There had been no talk of tumbling the roof, nor of setting flame to the thatch as Joly had ordered.

And the cabin stood still, unscathed, the half-door open at the top as always—the wrecking crew had not tumbled it. It sat in a tiny patch of a third of an acre, the turf pile almost emptied down to the ground, and the lazy-bed where the potatoes should be growing was bare and untilled. We had eaten our few seed potatoes long before planting time had come.

It was a good cabin, nearly watertight, with real thatch in places, and Joly's estate man had broken the rules and given it to a new family—they must have had a few coins set aside to square him.

Through the half-door I could see a woman and a man inside. Two children sprawled in the ash of the hearth, too young for field-work, and the woman's belly was swelling large under her apron.

"God be with you," I called quietly.

The woman looked up, saying "God and Mary be with you," before swallowing suddenly and turning to tug her husband's sleeve.

"Jesus, get away from the door." His face was hard and gaunt, there wasn't much more flesh on him than on myself. "Get away, you're not welcome here, spreading disease among decent people."

"I'm fine, I swear it to God and his mother. There's not a hint of a sickness on me. Just the hunger, is all."

I turned to the woman and begged. "For the love of God, this was my only home this twelve years past, I just came for a few things."

She grabbed a broom of twigs bound to a long ashplant as a handle, and waved it at me. "There's nothing left of your people here. I burned the lot of it. Why would I keep the oul' rags and dirt of the typhus house? Sure, it's a miracle the house itself is still standing."

"But the knife, maybe? My mother had a knife, for cutting the seed potatoes into quarters. It was wooden-handled and sharpened over the years into the shape of the crescent moon. You wouldn't burn a knife."

"It's gone." But she slipped her hand into her apron pocket, and I knew she was lying . . .